THE JUNIOR GREAT BOOKS

DISCUSSION PROGRAM

JUNIOR GREAT BOOKS

A Program of Interpretive Reading
and Discussion

Series Four, Volume One

EDITED BY
Richard P. Dennis and Edwin P. Moldof

THE GREAT BOOKS FOUNDATION

© *Copyright 1975 by* THE GREAT BOOKS FOUNDATION
Chicago, Illinois

published and distributed by

THE GREAT BOOKS FOUNDATION
a nonprofit corporation
307 North Michigan Avenue,
Chicago, Illinois 60601

ACKNOWLEDGMENTS

The Great Books Foundation wishes to thank the following publishers, authors and literary agencies for permission to reprint the material in this Junior Great Books series:

Thomas Y. Crowell Company, for "Fresh," from WHAT THE NEIGHBORS DID AND OTHER STORIES, copyright © 1959, 1967, 1972, by Philippa Pearce.

Doubleday & Company, Inc., for THE RED BALLOON, copyright © 1956, by A. Lamorisse.

Holt, Rinehart and Winston, Inc. for "Messenger to Maftam" and "The Cow-Tail Switch," from THE COW-TAIL SWITCH AND OTHER WEST AFRICAN STORIES, copyright 1948, by Harold Courlander & George Herzog.

J.B. Lippincott Co., Philadelphia and New York, for "The Story of Dr. Dolittle," copyright 1948 by Josephine Lofting. Copyright 1920 by Hugh Lofting. All rights reserved, including that of translation into foreign languages. This edition printed by special arrangement with J.B. Lippincott Co., Philadelphia and New York, publishers of the Doctor Doolittle series.

Meredith Press, for "Ali Baba and the Forty Thieves," copyright 1964, edited by Dr. Hedwig Smola. Translated by Charlotte Dixon.

Harold Ober Associates, for "The Goldfish," from THE LITTLE BOOKROOM, copyright 1955 by Eleanor Farjeon.

The New American Library of World Literature, Inc., New York, for "Fables," copyright 1962 by Ann Dunnigan, from FABLES AND FAIRY TALES by Leo Tolstoy, translated by Ann Dunnigan. Published by arrangement with The New American Library of World Literature, Inc., New York.

Helen Thurber, for "Fables," copyright 1940 by James Thurber. Copyright 1968 by Helen Thurber. From FABLES FOR OUR TIME, published by Harper & Row. Originally printed in THE NEW YORKER.

Thomas Yoseloff of A.S. Barnes & Company, Inc. for "The Little Humpbacked Horse" and "Vasilissa the Beautiful," from RUSSIAN WONDER TALES copyright 1912 by The Century Co. Copyright 1940 by Post Wheeler. Revised edition, copyright 1946, by Post Wheeler. New edition 1947.

CONTENTS

The Happy Prince *Oscar Wilde*	1
The Devoted Friend *Oscar Wilde*	17
Just So Stories *Rudyard Kipling*	36
The Messenger to Maftam *Harold Courlander & George Herzog*	60
The Cow-Tail Switch *Harold Courlander & George Herzog*	68
Fables *Aesop*	75
Fables for Our Time *James Thurber*	91
The Story of Doctor Dolittle *Hugh Lofting*	99
The Goldfish *Eleanor Farjeon*	162
A Short Course on Interpretive Reading, *Part One*	171

THE HAPPY PRINCE AND OTHER TALES

THE HAPPY PRINCE

HIGH ABOVE the city, on a tall column, stood the statue of the Happy Prince. He was gilded all over with thin leaves of fine gold, for eyes he had two bright sapphires, and a large red ruby glowed on his sword-hilt.

He was very much admired, indeed. "He is as beautiful as a weathercock," remarked one of the Town Councillors who wished to gain a reputation for having artistic tastes; "only not quite so useful," he added, fearing lest people should think him unpractical, which he really was not.

"Why can't you be like the Happy Prince?" asked a sensible mother of her little boy who was crying for the moon. "The Happy Prince never dreams of crying for anything."

"I am glad there is someone in the world who is quite happy," muttered a disappointed man as he gazed at the wonderful statue.

"He looks just like an angel," said the Charity

Children as they came out of the cathedral in their bright scarlet cloaks, and their clean white pinafores.

"How do you know?" said the Mathematical Master, "you have never seen one."

"Ah! but we have, in our dreams," answered the children; and the Mathematical Master frowned and looked very severe, for he did not approve of children dreaming.

One night there flew over the city a little Swallow. His friends had gone away to Egypt six weeks before, but he had stayed behind, for he was in love with the most beautiful Reed. He had met her early in the spring as he was flying down the river after a big yellow moth, and had been so attracted by her slender waist that he had stopped to talk to her.

"Shall I love you?" said the Swallow, who liked to come to the point at once, and the Reed made him a low bow. So he flew round and round her, touching the water with his wings, and making silver ripples. This was his courtship, and it lasted all through the summer.

"It is a ridiculous attachment," twittered the other Swallows, "she has no money, and far too many relations;" and, indeed, the river was quite full of Reeds. Then, when the autumn came, they all flew away.

The Happy Prince

After they had gone he felt lonely, and began to tire of his lady-love. "She has no conversation," he said, "and I am afraid that she is a coquette, for she is always flirting with the wind." And certainly, whenever the wind blew, the Reed made the most graceful curtsies. "I admit that she is domestic," he continued, "but I love travelling, and my wife, consequently, should love travelling also."

"Will you come away with me?" he said finally to her; but the Reed shook her head, she was so attached to her home.

"You have been trifling with me," he cried. "I am off to the Pyramids. Good-bye!" and he flew away.

All day long he flew, and at night-time he arrived at the city. "Where shall I put up?" he said; "I hope the town has made preparations."

Then he saw the statue on the tall column. "I will put up there," he cried; "it is a fine position with plenty of fresh air." So he alighted just between the feet of the Happy Prince.

"I have a golden bedroom," he said softly to himself as he looked round, and he prepared to go to sleep; but just as he was putting his head under his wing a large drop of water fell on him. "What a curious thing!" he cried, "there is not a single cloud in the sky, the stars are quite clear and bright, and yet it is raining. The climate in the north of Europe is really dreadful. The Reed used to like the rain, but that was merely her selfishness."

Then another drop fell.

"What is the use of a statue if it cannot keep the rain off?" he said; "I must look for a good chimney-pot," and he determined to fly away.

But before he had opened his wings, a third drop fell, and he looked up, and saw—Ah! what did he see?

The eyes of the Happy Prince were filled with tears, and tears were running down his golden cheeks. His face was so beautiful in the moonlight that the little Swallow was filled with pity.

"Who are you?" he said.

"I am the Happy Prince."

"Why are you weeping then?" asked the Swallow; "you have quite drenched me."

"When I was alive and had a human heart," answered the statue, "I did not know what tears were, for I lived in the Palace of Sans Souci, where sorrow is not allowed to enter. In the daytime I played with my companions in the garden, and in the evening I led the dance in the Great Hall. Round the garden ran a very lofty wall, but I never cared to ask what lay beyond it, everything about me was so beautiful. My courtiers called me the Happy Prince, and happy indeed I was, if pleasure be happiness. So I lived, and so I died. And now that I am dead they have set me up here so high that I can see all the ugliness and all the misery of my city, and though my heart is made of lead yet I cannot choose but weep."

"What, is he not solid gold?" said the Swallow to himself. He was too polite to make any personal remarks out loud.

"Far away," continued the statue in a low, musical voice, "far away in a little street there is a poor house. One of the windows is open, and through it I can see a woman seated at a table. Her face is thin and worn, and she has coarse red hands, all pricked by the needle, for she is a seamstress. She is embroidering passion-flowers on a satin gown for the loveliest of the Queen's maids-of-honour to wear at the next Court-ball. In a bed in the corner of the room her little boy is lying ill. He has a fever, and is asking for oranges. His mother has nothing to give him but river water, so he is crying. Swallow, Swallow, little Swallow, will you not bring her the ruby out of my sword-hilt? My feet are fastened to this pedestal and I cannot move."

"I am waited for in Egypt," said the Swallow. "My friends are flying up and down the Nile, and talking to the large lotus-flowers. Soon they will be going to sleep in the tomb of the great King. The

King is there himself in his painted coffin. He is wrapped in yellow linen, and embalmed with spices. Round his neck is a chain of pale green jade, and his hands are like withered leaves."

"Swallow, Swallow, little Swallow," said the Prince, "will you not stay with me for one night, and be my messenger? The boy is so thirsty, and the mother so sad."

"I don't think I like boys," answered the Swallow. "Last summer, when I was staying on the river, there were two rude boys, the miller's sons, who were always throwing stones at me. They never hit me, of course; we swallows fly far too well for that, and besides, I come of a family famous for its agility; but still, it was a mark of disrespect."

But the Happy Prince looked so sad that the little Swallow was sorry. "It is very cold here," he said; "but I will stay with you for one night, and be your messenger."

"Thank you, little Swallow," said the Prince.

So the Swallow picked out the great ruby from the Prince's sword, and flew away with it in his beak over the roofs of the town.

He passed by the cathedral tower, where the white marble angels were sculptured. He passed by the palace and heard the sound of dancing. A beautiful girl came out on the balcony with her lover.

"How wonderful the stars are," he said to her, "and how wonderful is the power of love!" "I hope my dress will be ready in time for the State-ball," she answered; "I have ordered passion-flowers to be embroidered on it; but the seamstresses are so lazy."

He passed over the river, and saw the lanterns hanging to the masts of the ships. He passed over the Ghetto, and saw the old Jews bargaining with each other, and weighing out money in copper scales. At last he came to the poor house and looked in. The boy was tossing feverishly on his bed, and the mother had fallen asleep, she was so tired. In he hopped, and laid the great ruby on the table beside the woman's thimble. Then he flew gently round the bed, fanning the boy's forehead with his wings. "How cool I feel," said the boy, "I must be getting better;" and he sank into a delicious slumber.

Then the Swallow flew back to the Happy Prince and told him what he had done. "It is curious," he remarked, "but I feel quite warm now, although it is so cold."

"That is because you have done a good action," said the Prince. And the little Swallow began to think, and then he fell asleep. Thinking always made him sleepy.

When day broke he flew down to the river and

had a bath. "What a remarkable phenomenon," said the Professor of Ornithology as he was passing over the bridge. "A swallow in winter!" And he wrote a long letter about it to the local newspaper. Every one quoted it, it was full of so many words that they could not understand.

"To-night I go to Egypt," said the Swallow, and he was in high spirits at the prospect. He visited all the public monuments, and sat a long time on top of the church steeple. Wherever he went the sparrows chirruped, and said to each other, "What a distinguished stranger!" so he enjoyed himself very much.

When the moon rose he flew back to the Happy Prince. "Have you any commissions for Egypt?" he cried. "I am just starting."

"Swallow, Swallow, little Swallow," said the Prince, "will you not stay with me one night longer?"

"I am waited for in Egypt," answered the Swallow. "Tomorrow my friends will fly up to the Second Cataract. The river-horse couches there among the bulrushes, and on a great granite throne sits the God Memmon. All night long he watches the stars, and when the morning star shines he utters one cry of joy, and then he is silent. At noon the yellow lions come down to the water's edge to drink. They have eyes like green beryls, and their roar is louder than the roar of the cataract."

"Swallow, Swallow, little Swallow," said the Prince, "far away across the city I see a young man in a garret. He is leaning over a desk covered with papers, and in a tumbler by his side there is a bunch of withered violets. His hair is brown and crisp, and his lips are red as a pomegranate, and he has large and dreamy eyes. He is trying to finish a play for the Director of the Theatre, but he is too cold to write any more. There is no fire in the grate, and hunger has made him faint."

"I will wait with you one night longer," said the Swallow, who really had a good heart. "Shall I take him another ruby?"

"Alas! I have no ruby now," said the Prince; "my eyes are all that I have left. They are made of rare sapphires, which were brought out of India a thousand years ago. Pluck out one of them and take it to him. He will sell it to the jeweller, and buy food and firewood, and finish his play."

"Dear Prince," said the Swallow, "I cannot do that;" and he began to weep.

"Swallow, Swallow, little Swallow," said the Prince, "do as I command you."

So the Swallow plucked out the Prince's eye, and flew away to the student's garret. It was easy enough to get in, as there was a hole in the roof. Through this he darted, and came into the room. The young man had his head buried in his hands, so he did not hear the flutter of the bird's wings, and when he looked up he found the beautiful sapphire lying on the withered violets.

"I am beginning to be appreciated," he cried; "this is from some great admirer. Now I can finish my play," and he looked quite happy.

The next day the Swallow flew down to the harbour. He sat on the mast of a large vessel and watched the sailors hauling big chests out of the hold with ropes. "Heave a-hoy!" they shouted as each chest came up. "I am going to Egypt!" cried the Swallow, but nobody minded, and when the moon rose he flew back to the Happy Prince.

"I am come to bid you good-bye," he cried.

"Swallow, Swallow, little Swallow," said the Prince, "will you not stay with me one night longer?"

"It is winter," answered the Swallow, "and the chill snow will soon be here. In Egypt the sun is warm on the green palm-trees, and the crocodiles lie in the mud and look lazily about them. My companions are building a nest in the Temple of Baalbec, and the pink and white doves are watching them, and cooing to each other. Dear Prince, I must leave you, but I will never forget you, and next spring I will bring you back two beautiful jewels in place of those you have given away. The ruby shall be redder than a red rose, and the sapphire shall be as blue as the great sea."

"In the square below," said the Happy Prince, "there stands a little match-girl. She has let her matches fall in the gutter, and they are all spoiled. Her father will beat her if she does not bring home some money, and she is crying. She has no shoes or stockings, and her little head is bare. Pluck out my other eye, and give it to her, and her father will not beat her."

"I will stay with you one night longer," said the Swallow, "but I cannot pluck out your eye. You would be quite blind then."

"Swallow, Swallow, little Swallow," said the Prince, "do as I command you."

So he plucked out the Prince's other eye, and darted down with it. He swooped past the match-girl, and slipped the jewel into the palm of her hand. "What a lovely bit of glass," cried the little girl; and she ran home, laughing.

Then the Swallow came back to the Prince. "You are blind now," he said, "so I will stay with you always."

"No, little Swallow," said the poor Prince, "you must go away to Egypt."

"I will stay with you always," said the Swallow, and he slept at the Prince's feet.

All the next day he sat on the Prince's shoulder, and told him stories of what he had seen in strange lands. He told him of the red ibises, who stand in long rows on the banks of the Nile, and catch gold fish in their beaks; of the Sphinx, who is as old as the world itself, and lives in the desert, and knows everything; of the merchants, who walk slowly by the side of their camels, and carry amber beads in their hands; of the King of the Mountains of the Moon, who is as black as ebony, and worships a large crystal; of the great green snake that sleeps in a palm-tree, and has twenty priests to feed it with honey-cakes; and of the pygmies who sail over a big lake on large flat leaves, and are always at war with the butterflies.

"Dear little Swallow," said the Prince, "you tell me of marvellous things, but more marvellous than anything is the suffering of men and of women. There is no Mystery so great as Misery. Fly over my city, little Swallow, and tell me what you see there."

The Happy Prince

So the Swallow flew over the great city, and saw the rich making merry in their beautiful houses, while the beggars were sitting at the gates. He flew into dark lanes, and saw the white faces of starving children looking out listlessly at the black streets. Under the archway of a bridge two little boys were lying in one another's arms to try and keep themselves warm. "How hungry we are!" they said. "You must not lie here," shouted the Watchman, and they wandered out into the rain.

Then he flew back and told the Prince what he had seen.

"I am covered with fine gold," said the Prince, "you must take it off, leaf by leaf, and give it to my poor; the living always think that gold can make them happy."

Leaf after leaf of the fine gold the Swallow picked off, till the Happy Prince looked quite dull and grey. Leaf after leaf of the fine gold he brought to the poor, and the children's faces grew rosier, and they laughed and played games in the street. "We have bread now!" they cried.

Then the snow came, and after the snow came the frost. The streets looked as if they were made of silver, they were so bright and glistening; long icicles like crystal daggers hung down from the eaves of the houses, everybody went about in furs, and the little boys wore scarlet caps and skated on the ice.

The poor little Swallow grew colder and colder, but he would not leave the Prince, he loved him too well. He picked up crumbs outside the baker's door when the baker was not looking, and tried to keep himself warm by flapping his wings.

But at last he knew that he was going to die. He had just strength to fly up to the Prince's shoulder once more. "Good-bye, dear Prince!" he murmured, "will you let me kiss your hand?"

"I am glad that you are going to Egypt at last, little Swallow," said the Prince, "you have stayed too long here; but you must kiss me on the lips, for I love you."

"It is not to Egypt that I am going," said the Swallow. "I am going to the House of Death. Death is the brother of Sleep, is he not?"

And he kissed the Happy Prince on the lips, and fell down dead at his feet.

At that moment a curious crack sounded inside the statue, as if something had broken. The fact is that the leaden heart had snapped right in two. It certainly was a dreadfully hard frost.

Early the next morning the Mayor was walking in the square below in company with the Town Councillors. As they passed the column he looked

The Happy Prince

up at the statue: "Dear me! how shabby the Happy Prince looks!" he said.

"How shabby indeed!" cried the Town Councillors, who always agreed with the Mayor, and they went up to look at it.

"The ruby has fallen out of his sword, his eyes are gone, and he is golden no longer," said the Mayor; "in fact, he is little better than a beggar!"

"Little better than a beggar," said the Town Councillors.

"And here is actually a dead bird at his feet!" continued the Mayor. "We must really issue a proclamation that birds are not to be allowed to die here." And the Town Clerk made a note of the suggestion.

So they pulled down the statue of the Happy Prince. "As he is no longer beautiful he is no longer useful," said the Art Professor at the University.

Then they melted the statue in a furnace, and the Mayor held a meeting of the Corporation to decide what was to be done with the metal. "We must have another statue, of course," he said, "and it shall be a statue of myself."

"Of myself," said each of the Town Councillors, and they quarrelled. When I last heard of them they were quarrelling still.

"What a strange thing," said the overseer of the workmen at the foundry. "This broken lead heart will not melt in the furnace. We must throw it away." So they threw it on a dust heap where the dead Swallow was also lying.

"Bring me the two most precious things in the city," said God to one of His Angels; and the Angel brought Him the leaden heart and the dead bird.

"You have rightly chosen," said God, "for in my garden of Paradise this little bird shall sing for evermore, and in my city of gold the Happy Prince shall praise me."

THE DEVOTED FRIEND

ONE MORNING the old Water-rat put his head out of his hole. He had bright beady eyes and stiff grey whiskers, and his tail was like a long bit of black india-rubber. The little ducks were swimming about in the pond, looking just like a lot of yellow canaries, and their mother, who was pure white with real red legs, was trying to teach them how to stand on their heads in the water.

"You will never be in the best society unless you can stand on your heads," she kept saying to them; and every now and then she showed them how it was done. But the little ducks paid no attention to her. They were so young that they did not know what an advantage it is to be in society at all.

"What disobedient children!" cried the old Water-rat; "they really deserve to be drowned."

"Nothing of the kind," answered the Duck; "every one must make a beginning, and parents cannot be too patient."

"Ah! I know nothing about the feelings of parents," said the Water-rat; "I am not a family man.

In fact, I have never been married, and I never intend to be. Love is all very well in its way, but friendship is much higher. Indeed, I know of nothing in the world that is either nobler or rarer than a devoted friendship."

"And what, pray, is your idea of the duties of a devoted friend?" asked a Green Linnet, who was sitting in a willow-tree hard by, and had overheard the conversation.

"Yes, that is just what I want to know," said the Duck, and she swam away to the end of the pond, and stood upon her head, in order to give her children a good example.

"What a silly question!" cried the Water-rat. "I should expect my devoted friend to be devoted to me, of course."

"And what would you do in return?" said the little bird, swinging upon a silver spray, and flapping his tiny wings.

"I don't understand you," answered the Water-rat.

"Let me tell you a story on the subject," said the Linnet.

"Is the story about me?" asked the Water-rat. "If so, I will listen to it, for I am extremely fond of fiction."

"It is applicable to you," answered the Linnet;

The Devoted Friend

and he flew down, and alighting upon the bank, he told the story of The Devoted Friend.

"Once upon a time," said the Linnet, "there was an honest little fellow named Hans."

"Was he very distinguished?" asked the Water-rat.

"No," answered the Linnet, "I don't think he was distinguished at all, except for his kind heart, and his funny round good-humoured face. He lived in a tiny cottage all by himself, and every day he worked in his garden. In all the country-side there was no garden so lovely as his. Sweet-william grew there, and Gilly-flowers, and Shepherd's-purses, and Fair-maids of France. There were damask Roses, and yellow Roses, lilac Crocuses, and gold, purple Violets and white. Columbine and Lady-smock, Marjoram and Wild Basil, the Cowslip and the Flower-de-luce, the Daffodil and the Clove-Pink bloomed or blossomed in their proper order as the months went by, one flower taking another flower's place, so that there were always beautiful things to look at, and pleasant odours to smell.

"Little Hans had a great many friends, but the most devoted friend of all was big Hugh the Miller. Indeed, so devoted was the rich Miller to little Hans, that he would never go by his garden without leaning over the wall and plucking a large nosegay, or a handful of sweet herbs, or filling his pockets with plums and cherries if it was the fruit season.

" 'Real friends should have everything in common' the Miller used to say, and little Hans nodded and smiled, and felt very proud of having a friend with such noble ideas.

"Sometimes, indeed, the neighbours thought it strange that the rich Miller never gave little Hans anything in return, though he had a hundred sacks of flour stored away in his mill, and six milch cows, and a large flock of woolly sheep; but Hans never troubled his head about these things, and nothing gave him greater pleasure than to listen to all the wonderful things the Miller used to say about the unselfishness of true friendship.

"So little Hans worked away in his garden. During the spring, the summer, and the autumn he was very happy, but when winter came, and he had no fruit or flowers to bring to the market, he suffered a good deal from cold and hunger, and often had to go to bed without any supper but a few dried pears or some hard nuts. In the winter, also, he was extremely lonely, as the Miller never came to see him then.

" 'There is no good in my going to see little Hans as long as the snow lasts,' the Miller used to say to his wife, 'for when people are in trouble they should be left alone, and not be bothered by visitors. That at least is my idea about friendship, and I am sure I am right. So I shall wait till the spring comes, and then I shall pay him a visit, and he will be able to give me a large basket of primroses, and that will make him so happy.'

" 'You are certainly very thoughtful about others,' answered the Wife, as she sat in her comfortable armchair by the big pinewood fire; 'very thoughtful indeed. It is quite a treat to hear you talk about friendship. I am sure the clergyman himself could not say such beautiful things as you do, though he does live in a three-storied house, and wear a gold ring on his little finger.'

" 'But could we not ask little Hans up here?' said the Miller's youngest son. 'If poor Hans is in trouble I will give him half my porridge, and show him my white rabbits.'

" 'What a silly boy you are!' cried the Miller; 'I really don't know what is the use of sending you to school. You seem not to learn anything. Why, if little Hans came up here, and saw our warm fire, and our good supper, and our great cask of red wine, he might get envious, and envy is a most terrible thing, and would spoil anybody's nature. I certainly will not allow Hans's nature to be spoiled. I am his best friend, and I will always watch over him, and see that he is not led into any temptations. Besides, if Hans came here, he might ask me to let him have some flour on credit, and that I could not do. Flour is one thing, and friendship is another, and they should not be confused. Why, the words are spelt differently, and mean quite different things. Everybody can see that.'

" 'How well you talk!' said the Miller's Wife, pouring herself out a large glass of warm ale; 'really I feel quite drowsy. It is just like being in church.'

" 'Lots of people act well,' answered the Miller; 'but very few people talk well, which shows that talking is much the more difficult thing of the two, and much the finer thing also;' and he looked sternly across the table at his little son, who felt so ashamed of himself that he hung his head down, and grew quite scarlet, and began to cry into his tea. However, he was so young that you must excuse him."

"Is that the end of the story?" asked the Water-rat.

"Certainly not," answered the Linnet, "that is the beginning."

"Then you are quite behind the age," said the Water-rat. "Every good story-teller nowadays starts with the end, and then goes on to the beginning, and concludes with the middle. That is the new method. I heard all about it the other day from a critic who was walking round the pond with a young man. He spoke of the matter at great length, and I am sure he must have been right, for he had blue spectacles and a bald head, and whenever the young man made any remark, he always answered 'Pooh!' But pray go on with your story. I like the Miller immensely. I have all kinds of beautiful sentiments myself, so there is a great sympathy between us."

"Well," said the Linnet, hopping now on one leg and now on the other, "as soon as the winter was over, and the primroses began to open their pale yellow stars, the Miller said to his wife that he would go down and see little Hans.

" 'Why, what a good heart you have!' cried his Wife; 'you are always thinking of others. And mind you take the big basket with you for the flowers.'

"So the Miller tied the sails of the windmill together with a strong iron chain, and went down the hill with the basket on his arm.

" 'Good morning, little Hans,' said the Miller.

" 'Good morning,' said Hans, leaning on his spade, and smiling from ear to ear.

" 'And how have you been all the winter?' said the Miller.

" 'Well, really,' cried Hans, 'it is very good of you

to ask, very good indeed. I am afraid I had rather a hard time of it, but now the spring has come, and I am quite happy, and all my flowers are doing well.'

" 'We often talked of you during the winter, Hans,' said the Miller, 'and wondered how you were getting on.'

" 'That was kind of you,' said Hans; 'I was half afraid you had forgotten me.'

" 'Hans, I am surprised at you,' said the Miller; 'friendship never forgets. That is the wonderful thing about it, but I am afraid you don't understand the poetry of life. How lovely your primroses are looking, by-the-bye!'

" 'They are certainly very lovely,' said Hans, 'and it is a most lucky thing for me that I have so many. I am going to bring them into the market and sell them to the Burgomaster's daughter, and buy back my wheelbarrow with the money.'

" 'Buy back your wheelbarrow? You don't mean to say you have sold it? What a very stupid thing to do!'

" 'Well, the fact is,' said Hans, 'that I was obliged to. You see the winter was a very bad time for me, and I really had no money at all to buy bread with. So I first sold the silver buttons off my Sunday coat, and then I sold my silver chain, and then I sold my big pipe, and at last I sold my wheelbarrow. But I am going to buy them all back again now.'

" 'Hans,' said the Miller, 'I will give you my wheelbarrow. It is not in very good repair; indeed, one side is gone, and there is something wrong with the wheel-spokes; but in spite of that I will give it to you. I know it is very generous of me, and a great many people would think me extremely foolish for parting with it, but I am not like the rest of the world. I think that generosity is the essence of friendship, and, besides, I have got a new wheelbarrow for myself. Yes, you may set your mind at ease, I will give you my wheelbarrow.'

" 'Well, really, that is generous of you,' said little Hans, and his funny round face glowed all over with pleasure. 'I can easily put it in repair, as I have a plank of wood in the house.'

" 'A plank of wood!' said the Miller; 'why, that is just what I want for the roof of my barn. There is a very large hole in it, and the corn will all get damp if I don't stop it up. How lucky you mentioned it! It is remarkable how one good action always breeds another. I have given you my wheelbarrow, and now you are going to give me your plank. Of course, the wheelbarrow is worth far more than the plank, but the friendship never notices things like that. Pray get it at once, and I will set to work at my barn this very day.'

" 'Certainly,' cried little Hans, and he ran into the shed and dragged the plank out.

" 'It is not a very big plank,' said the Miller, looking at it, 'and I am afraid that after I have mended my barn-roof there won't be any left for you to mend the wheelbarrow with; but, of course, that is not my fault. And now, as I have given you my wheelbarrow, I am sure you would like to give me some flowers in return. Here is the basket, and mind you fill it quite full.'

" 'Quite full?' said little Hans, rather sorrowfully, for it was really a very big basket, and he knew that if he filled it he would have no flowers left for the market, and he was very anxious to get his silver buttons back.

" 'Well, really,' answered the Miller, 'as I have given you my wheelbarrow, I don't think that it is much to ask you for a few flowers. I may be wrong, but I should have thought that friendship, true friendship, was quite free from selfishness of any kind.'

" 'My dear friend, my best friend,' cried little Hans, 'you are welcome to all the flowers in my garden. I would much sooner have your good opinion than my silver buttons, any day,' and he ran and plucked all his pretty primroses, and filled the Miller's basket.

" 'Good-bye, little Hans,' said the Miller, as he went up the hill with the plank on his shoulder, and the big basket in his hand.

" 'Good-bye,' said little Hans, and he began to dig away quite merrily, he was so pleased about the wheelbarrow.

"The next day he was nailing up some honeysuckle against the porch, when he heard the Miller's voice calling to him from the road. So he jumped off the ladder, and ran down the garden, and looked over the wall.

"There was the Miller with a large sack of flour on his back.

" 'Dear little Hans,' said the Miller, 'would you mind carrying this sack of flour for me to market?'

" 'Oh, I am so sorry,' said Hans, 'but I am really very busy to-day. I have got all my creepers to nail up, and all my flowers to water, and all my grass to roll.'

" 'Well, really,' said the Miller, 'I think that, considering that I am going to give you my wheelbarrow, it is rather unfriendly of you to refuse.'

" 'Oh, don't say that,' cried little Hans, 'I

wouldn't be unfriendly for the whole world;' and he ran in for his cap, and trudged off with the big sack on his shoulders.

"It was a very hot day, and the road was terribly dusty, and before Hans had reached the sixth milestone he was so tired that he had to sit down and rest. However, he went on bravely, and at last he reached the market. After he had waited there some time, he sold the sack of flour for a very good price, and then he returned home at once, for he was afraid that if he stopped too late he might meet some robbers on the way.

" 'It has certainly been a hard day,' said little Hans to himself as he was going to bed, 'but I am glad I did not refuse the Miller, for he is my best friend, and, besides, he is going to give me his wheelbarrow.'

"Early the next morning the Miller came down to get the money for his sack of flour, but little Hans was so tired that he was still in bed.

" 'Upon my word,' said the Miller, 'you are very lazy. Really, considering that I am going to give you my wheelbarrow, I think you might work harder. Idleness is a great sin, and I certainly don't like any of my friends to be idle or sluggish. You must not mind my speaking quite plainly to you. Of course I should not dream of doing so if I were not

The Devoted Friend 29

your friend. But what is the good of friendship if one cannot say exactly what one means? Anybody can say charming things and try to please and to flatter, but a true friend always says unpleasant things, and does not mind giving pain. Indeed, if he is a really true friend he prefers it, for he knows that then he is doing good.'

" 'I am very sorry,' said little Hans, rubbing his eyes and pulling off his night cap, 'but I was so tired that I thought I would lie in bed for a little time, and listen to the birds singing. Do you know that I always work better after hearing the birds sing?'

" 'Well, I am glad of that,' said the Miller, clapping little Hans on the back, 'for I want you to come up to the mill as soon as you are dressed, and mend my barn-roof for me.'

"Poor little Hans was very anxious to go and work in his garden, for his flowers had not been watered for two days, but he did not like to refuse the Miller, as he was such a good friend to him.

" 'Do you think it would be unfriendly of me if I said I was busy?' he inquired in a shy and timid voice.

" 'Well, really,' answered the Miller, 'I do not think it is much to ask of you, considering that I am going to give you my wheelbarrow; but, of course if you refuse I will go and do it myself.'

" 'Oh! on no account,' cried little Hans; and he jumped out of bed, and dressed himself, and went up to the barn.

"He worked there all day long, till sunset, and at sunset the Miller came to see how he was getting on.

" 'Have you mended the hole in the roof yet, little Hans?' cried the Miller in a cheery voice.

" 'It is quite mended,' answered little Hans, coming down the ladder.

" 'Ah!' said the Miller, 'there is no work so delightful as the work one does for others.'

" 'It is certainly a great privilege to hear you talk,' answered little Hans, sitting down and wiping his forehead, 'a very great privilege. But I am afraid I shall never have such beautiful ideas as you have.'

" 'Oh! they will come to you,' said the Miller, 'but you must take more pains. At present you have only the practice of friendship; some day you will have the theory also.'

" 'Do you really think I shall?' asked little Hans.

" 'I have no doubt of it,' answered the Miller: 'but now that you have mended the roof, you had better go home and rest, for I want you to drive my sheep to the mountain tomorrow.'

"Poor little Hans was afraid to say anything to this, and early the next morning the Miller brought

The Devoted Friend

his sheep round to the cottage, and Hans started off with them to the mountain. It took him the whole day to get there and back; and when he returned he was so tired that he went off to sleep in his chair, and did not wake up till it was broad daylight.

" 'What a delightful time I shall have in my garden,' he said, and he went to work at once.

"But somehow he was never able to look after his flowers at all, for his friend the Miller was always coming round and sending him off on long errands, or getting him to help at the mill. Little Hans was very much distressed at times, as he was afraid his flowers would think he had forgotten them, but he consoled himself by the reflection that the Miller was his best friend. 'Besides,' he used to say, 'he is going to give me his wheelbarrow, and that is an act of pure generosity.'

"So little Hans worked away for the Miller, and the Miller said all kinds of beautiful things about friendship, which Hans took down in a note-book, and used to read over at night, for he was a very good scholar.

"Now it happened that one evening little Hans was sitting by his fireside when a loud rap came at the door. It was a very wild night, and the wind was blowing and roaring round the house so terribly that at first he thought it was merely the storm. But a second rap came, and then a third, louder than either of the others.

" 'It is some poor traveller,' said little Hans to himself, and he ran to the door.

"There stood the Miller with a lantern in one hand and a big stick in the other.

" 'Dear little Hans,' cried the Miller, 'I am in great trouble. My little boy has fallen off a ladder and hurt himself, and I am going for the Doctor. But he lives so far away, and it is such a bad night, that it has just occurred to me that it would be much better if you went instead of me. You know I am going to give you my wheelbarrow, and so it is only fair that you should do something for me in return.'

" 'Certainly,' cried little Hans, 'I take it quite as a compliment your coming to me, and I will start off at once. But you must lend me your lantern, as the night is so dark that I am afraid I might fall into the ditch.'

" 'I am very sorry,' answered the Miller, 'but it is my new lantern, and it would be a great loss to me if anything happened to it.'

" 'Well, never mind, I will do without it,' cried little Hans, and he took down his great fur coat, and his warm scarlet cap, and tied a muffler round his throat, and started off.

"What a dreadful night it was! The night was so black that little Hans could hardly see, and the wind was so strong that he could scarcely stand. However, he was very courageous, and after he had been walking about three hours, he arrived at the Doctor's house, and knocked at the door.

" 'Who is there?' cried the Doctor, putting his head out of his bedroom window.

" 'Little Hans, Doctor.'

" 'What do you want, little Hans?'

" 'The Milier's son has fallen from a ladder, and has hurt himself, and the Miller wants you to come at once.'

" 'All right!' said the Doctor; and he ordered his horse, and his big boots, and his lantern, and came downstairs, and rode off in the direction of the Miller's house, little Hans trudging behind him.

"But the storm grew worse and worse, and the rain fell in torrents, and little Hans could not see where he was going, or keep up with the horse. At last he lost his way, and wandered off on the moor, which was a very dangerous place, as it was full of deep holes, and there poor little Hans was drowned. His body was found the next day by some goatherds, floating in a great pool of water, and was brought back by them to the cottage.

"Everybody went to little Han's funeral, as he

was so popular, and the Miller was the chief mourner.

" 'As I was his best friend,' said the Miller, 'it is only fair that I should have the best place;' so he walked at the head of the procession in a long black cloak, and every now and then he wiped his eyes with a big pocket-handkerchief.

" 'Little Hans is certainly a great loss to every one,' said the Blacksmith, when the funeral was over, and they were all seated comfortably in the inn, drinking spiced wine and eating sweet cakes.

" 'A great loss to me at any rate,' answered the Miller: 'why, I had as good as given him my wheelbarrow, and now I really don't know what to do with it. It is very much in my way at home, and it is in such bad repair that I could not get anything for it if I sold it. I will certainly take care not to give away anything again. One always suffers for being generous.' "

"Well?" said the Water-rat, after a long pause.

"Well, that is the end," said the Linnet.

"But what became of the Miller?" asked the Water-rat.

"Oh! I really don't know," replied the Linnet; "and I am sure that I don't care."

"It is quite evident then that you have no sympathy in your nature," said the Water-rat.

"I am afraid you don't quite see the moral of the story," remarked the Linnet.

"The what?" screamed the Water-rat.

"The moral."

"Do you mean to say that the story has a moral?"

"Certainly," said the Linnet.

"Well, really," said the Water-rat, in a very angry manner, "I think you should have told me that before you began. If you had done so, I certainly would not have listened to you; in fact, I should have said 'Pooh,' like the critic. However, I can say it now;" so he shouted out "Pooh" at the top of his voice, gave a whisk with his tail, and went back into his hole.

"And how do you like the Water-rat?" asked the Duck, who came paddling up some minutes afterwards. "He has a great many good points, but for my own part I have a mother's feelings, and I can never look at a confirmed bachelor without the tears coming into my eyes."

"I am rather afraid that I have annoyed him," said the Linnet. "The fact is, that I told him a story with a moral."

"Ah! that is always a very dangerous thing to do," said the Duck.

And I quite agree with her.

JUST SO STORIES

HOW THE WHALE GOT HIS THROAT

IN THE SEA, once upon a time, O my Best Beloved, there was a Whale, and he ate fishes. He ate the starfish and the garfish, and the crab and the dab, and the plaice and the dace, and the skate and his mate, and the mackereel and the pickereel, and the really truly twirly-whirly eel. All the fishes he could find in all the sea he ate with his mouth—so! Till at last there was only one small fish left in all the sea, and he was a small 'Stute Fish, and he swam a little behind the Whale's right ear, so as to be out of harm's way. Then the Whale stood up on his tail and said, "I'm hungry." And the small 'Stute Fish said in a small 'stute voice, "Noble and generous Cetacean, have you ever tasted Man?"

"No," said the Whale. "What is it like?"

"Nice," said the small 'Stute Fish. "Nice but nubbly."

"Then fetch me some," said the Whale, and he made the sea froth up with his tail.

"One at a time is enough," said the 'Stute Fish. "If you swim to latitude Fifty North, longitude

How the Whale Got His Throat

Forty West (that is magic), you will find, sitting *on* a raft, *in* the middle of the sea, with nothing on but a pair of blue canvas breeches, a pair of suspenders (you must *not* forget the suspenders, Best Beloved), and a jack-knife, one shipwrecked Mariner, who, it is only fair to tell you, is a man of infinite-resource-and-sagacity."

So the Whale swam and swam to latitude Fifty North, longitude Forty West, as fast as he could swim, and *on* a raft, *in* the middle of the sea, *with* nothing to wear except a pair of blue canvas breeches, a pair of suspenders (you must particularly remember the suspenders, Best Beloved), *and* a jack-knife, he found one single, solitary shipwrecked Mariner, trailing his toes in the water. (He had his mummy's leave to paddle, or else he would never have done it, because he was a man of infinite-resource-and-sagacity.)

Then the Whale opened his mouth back and back and back till it nearly touched his tail, and he swallowed the shipwrecked Mariner, and the raft he was sitting on, and his blue canvas breeches, and the suspenders (which you *must* not forget), *and* the jack-knife—He swallowed them all down into his warm, dark, inside cupboards, and then he smacked his lips—so, and turned round three times on his tail.

But as soon as the Mariner, who was a man of infinite-resource-and-sagacity, found himself truly inside the Whale's warm, dark, inside cupboards, he stumped and he jumped and he thumped and he bumped, and he pranced and he danced, and he banged and he clanged, and he hit and he bit, and he leaped and he creeped, and he prowled and he howled, and he hopped and he dropped, and he cried and he sighed, and he crawled and he bawled, and he stepped and he lepped, and he danced hornpipes where he shouldn't, and the Whale felt most unhappy indeed. (*Have* you forgotten the suspenders?)

So he said to the 'Stute Fish, "This man is very nubbly, and besides he is making me hiccough. What shall I do?"

"Tell him to come out," said the 'Stute Fish.

So the Whale called down his own throat to the shipwrecked Mariner, "Come out and behave yourself. I've got the hiccoughs."

"Nay, nay!" said the Mariner. "Not so, but far otherwise. Take me to my natal-shore and the white-cliffs-of-Albion, and I'll think about it." And he began to dance more than ever.

"You had better take him home," said the 'Stute Fish to the Whale. "I ought to have warned you that he is a man of infinite-resource-and-sagacity."

So the Whale swam and swam and swam, with both flippers and his tail, as hard as he could for the hiccoughs; and at last he saw the Mariner's natal-shore and the white-cliffs-of-Albion, and he rushed half-way up the beach and opened his mouth wide and wide and wide, and said, "Change here for Winchester, Ashuelot, Nashua, Keene, and stations on the *Fitch*burg Road." And just as he said "Fitch" the Mariner walked out of his mouth. But while the Whale had been swimming, the Mariner, who was indeed a person of infinite-resource-and-sagacity, had taken his jack-knife and cut up the raft into a little square grating all running criss-cross, and he had tied it firm with his suspenders (*now* you know why you were not to forget the suspenders!), and he dragged that grating good and tight into the Whale's throat, and there it stuck! Then he recited the following Sloka, which, as you have not heard it, I will now proceed to relate—

> By means of a grating
> I have stopped your ating.

For the Mariner he was also an Hi-ber-ni-an. And he stepped out on the shingle, and went home to his mother, who had given him leave to trail his toes in the water; and he married and lived happily ever afterward. So did the Whale. But from that day on, the grating in his throat, which he could neither cough up nor swallow down, prevented him eating anything except very, very small fish; and this is the reason why whales nowadays never eat men or boys or little girls.

The small 'Stute Fish went and hid himself in the mud under the Door-sills of the Equator. He was afraid that the Whale might be angry with him.

The Sailor took the jack-knife home. He was wearing the blue canvas breeches when he walked out on the shingle. The suspenders were left behind, you see, to tie that grating with; and that is the end of *that* tale.

When the cabin port-holes are dark and green
    Because of the seas outside;
When the ship goes *wop* (with a wiggle between)
And the steward falls into the soup-tureen,
    And the trunks begin to slide;
When Nursey lies on the floor in a heap,
And Mummy tells you to let her sleep,
And you aren't waked or washed or dressed,
Why, then you will know (if you haven't guessed)
You're "Fifty North and Forty West!"

HOW THE CAMEL GOT HIS HUMP

Now this is the next tale, and it tells how the Camel got his big hump.

In the beginning of years, when the world was so new and all, and the Animals were just beginning to work for Man, there was a Camel, and he lived in the middle of a Howling Desert because he did not want to work; and besides, he was a Howler himself. So he ate sticks and thorns and tamarisks and milkweed and prickles, most 'scruciating idle; and when anybody spoke to him he said "Humph!" Just "Humph!" and no more.

Presently the Horse came to him on Monday morning, with a saddle on his back and a bit in his mouth, and said, "Camel, O Camel, come out and trot like the rest of us."

"Humph!" said the Camel and the Horse went away and told the Man.

Presently the Dog came to him, with a stick in his mouth, and said, "Camel, O Camel, come and fetch and carry like the rest of us."

"Humph!" said the Camel; and the Dog went away and told the Man.

Presently the Ox came to him, with the yoke on his neck and said, "Camel, O Camel, come and plough like the rest of us."

"Humph!" said the Camel; and the Ox went away and told the Man.

At the end of the day the Man called the Horse and the Dog and the Ox together, and said, "Three, O Three, I'm very sorry for you (with the world so new-and-all); but that Humph-thing in the Desert can't work, or he would have been here by now, so I am going to leave him alone, and you must work double-time to make up for it."

That made the Three very angry (with the world so new-and-all), and they held a palaver, and an *indaba,* and a *punchayet,* and a pow-wow on the edge of the Desert; and the Camel came chewing milkweed *most* 'scruciating idle, and laughed at them. Then he said "Humph!" and went away again.

Presently there came along the Djinn in charge of All Deserts, rolling in a cloud of dust (Djinns always travel that way because it is Magic), and he stopped to palaver and pow-wow with the Three.

"Djinn of All Deserts," said the Horse, *"is* it right

for any one to be idle, with the world so new-and-all?"

"Certainly not," said the Djinn.

"Well," said the Horse, "there's a thing in the middle of your Howling Desert (and he's a Howler himself) with a long neck and long legs, and he hasn't done a stroke of work since Monday morning. He won't trot."

"Whew!" said the Djinn, whistling, "that's my Camel, for all the gold in Arabia! What does he say about it?"

"He says 'Humph!'" said the Dog; "and he won't fetch and carry."

"Does he say anything else?"

"Only 'Humph!'; and he won't plough," said the Ox.

"Very good," said the Djinn. "I'll humph him if you will kindly wait a minute."

The Djinn rolled himself up in his dustcloak, and took a bearing across the desert, and found the Camel most 'scruciatingly idle, looking at his own reflection in a pool of water.

"My long and bubbling friend," said the Djinn, "what's this I hear of your doing no work, with the world so new-and-all?"

"Humph!" said the Camel.

The Djinn sat down, with his chin in his hand, and began to think a Great Magic, while the Camel looked at his own reflection in the pool of water.

"You've given the Three extra work ever since Monday morning, all on account of your 'scruciating idleness," said the Djinn; and he went on thinking Magics, with his chin in his hand.

"Humph!" said the Camel.

"I shouldn't say that again if I were you," said the Djinn; "you might say it once too often. Bubbles, I want you to work."

And the Camel said "Humph!" again; but no sooner had he said it than he saw his back, that he was so proud of, puffing up and puffing up into a great big lolloping humph.

"Do you see that?" said the Djinn. "That's your very own humph that you've brought upon your very own self by not working. To-day is Thursday, and you've done no work since Monday, when the work began. Now you are going to work."

"How can I," said the Camel, "with this humph on my back?"

"That's made a-purpose," said the Djinn, "all because you missed those three days. You will be able to work now for three days without eating, because you can live on your humph; and don't you ever say

I never did anything for you. Come out of the Desert and go to the Three, and behave. Humph yourself!"

And the Camel humphed himself, humph and all, and went away to join the Three. And from that day to this the Camel always wears a humph (we call it "hump" now, not to hurt his feelings); but he has never yet caught up with the three days that he missed at the beginning of the world, and he has never yet learned how to behave.

The Camel's hump is an ugly lump
    Which well you may see at the Zoo;
But uglier yet is the hump we get
    From having too little to do.

Kiddies and grown-ups too-oo-oo,
If we haven't enough to do-oo-oo,
    We get the hump—
    Cameelious hump—
The hump that is black and blue!

We climb out of bed with a frouzly head
    And a snarly-yarly voice.
We shiver and scowl and we grunt and we growl
    At our bath and our boots and our toys;

And there ought to be a corner for me
(And I know there is one for you)
    When we get the hump—
    Cameelious hump—
The hump that is black and blue!

The cure for this ill is not to sit still,
    Or frowst with a book by the fire;
But to take a large hoe and a shovel also,
    And dig till you gently perspire.

And then you will find that the sun and the wind
And the Djinn of the Garden too,
    Have lifted the hump—
    The horrible hump—
The hump that is black and blue!

I get it as well as you-oo-oo—
If I haven't enough to do-oo-oo—
    We all get hump—
    Cameelious hump—
Kiddies and grown-ups too!

THE ELEPHANT'S CHILD

IN THE HIGH and Far-Off times the Elephant, O Best Beloved, had no trunk. He had only a blackish, bulgy nose, as big as a boot that he could wriggle about from side to side; but he couldn't pick up things with it. But there was one Elephant—a new Elephant—an Elephant's Child—who was full of 'satiable curtiosity, and that means he asked ever so many questions. *And* he lived in Africa, and he filled all Africa with his 'satiable curtiosities. He asked his tall aunt, the Ostrich, why her tailfeathers grew just so, and his tall aunt the Ostrich spanked him with her hard, hard claw. He asked his tall uncle, the Giraffe, what made his skin spotty, and his tall uncle, the Giraffe spanked him with his hard, hard hoof. And still he was full of 'satiable curtiosity! He asked his broad aunt, the Hippopotamus, why her eyes were red, and his broad aunt, the Hippopotamus, spanked him with her broad, broad hoof; and he asked his hairy uncle, the Baboon, why melons tasted just so, and his hairy uncle, the Baboon, spanked him with his hairy, hairy paw.

And *still* he was full of 'satiable curtiosity! He asked questions about everything that he saw, or heard, or felt, or smelt, or touched, and all his uncles and his aunts spanked him. And still he was full of 'satiable curtiosity!

One fine morning in the middle of the Precession of the Equinoxes this 'satiable Elephant's Child asked a new fine question that he had never asked before. He asked, "What does the Crocodile have for dinner?" Then everybody said, "Hush!" in a loud and dretful tone, and they spanked him immediately and directly, without stopping, for a long time.

By and by, when that was finished, he came upon Kolokolo Bird sitting in the middle of a wait-a-bit thorn-bush, and he said, "My father has spanked me, and my mother has spanked me; all my aunts and uncles have spanked me for my 'satiable curtiosity; and *still* I want to know what the Crocodile has for dinner!"

Then Kolokolo Bird said, with a mournful cry, "Go to the banks of the great grey-green, greasy Limpopo River, all set about with fever-trees, and find out."

That very next morning, when there was nothing left of the Equinoxes, because the Precession had preceded according to precedent this 'satiable Ele-

The Elephant's Child

phant's Child took a hundred pounds of bananas (the little short red kind), and a hundred pounds of sugarcane (the long purple kind), and seventeen melons (the greeny-crackly kind), and said to all his dear families, "Good-bye. I am going to the great grey-green, greasy Limpopo River, all set about with fever-trees, to find out what the Crocodile has for dinner." And they all spanked him once more for luck, though he asked them most politely to stop.

Then he went away, a little warm, but not at all astonished, eating melons, and throwing the rind about, because he could not pick it up.

He went from Graham's Town to Kimberley, and from Kimberley to Khama's Country, and from Khama's Country he went east and north, eating melons all the time, till he at last came to the banks of the great grey-green, greasy Limpopo River, all set about with fever-trees, precisely as Kolokolo Bird had said.

Now you must know and understand, O Best Beloved, that till that very week, and day, and hour, and minute, this 'satiable Elephant's Child had never seen a Crocodile, and did not know what one was like. It was all his 'satiable curtiosity.

The first thing that he found was a Bi-

Coloured-Python-Rock-Snake curled round a rock.

" 'Scuse me," said the Elephant's Child most politely, "but have you seen such a thing as a Crocodile in these promiscuous parts?"

"*Have* I seen a Crocodile?" said the Bi-Coloured-Python-Rock-Snake, in a voice of dretful scorn. "What will you ask me next?"

" 'Scuse me," said the Elephant's Child, "but could you kindly tell me what he has for dinner?"

Then the Bi-Coloured-Python-Rock-Snake uncoiled himself very quickly from the rock, and spanked the Elephant's Child with his scalesome, flailsome tail.

"That is odd," said the Elephant's Child, "because my father and my mother, and my uncle and my aunt, not to mention my other aunt, the Hippopotamus, and my other uncle, the Baboon, have all spanked me for my 'satiable curtiosity—and I suppose this is the same thing."

So he said good-bye very politely to the Bi-Coloured-Python-Rock-Snake, and helped to coil him up on the rock again, and went on, a little warm, but not at all astonished, eating melons, and throwing the rind about because he could not pick it up, till he trod on what he thought was a log of wood at the very edge of the great grey-green, greasy Limpopo River, all set about with fever-trees.

But it was really the Crocodile, O Best Beloved, and the Crocodile winked one eye—like this!

" 'Scuse me," said the Elephant's Child most politely, "but do you happen to have seen a Crocodile in these promiscuous parts?"

Then the Crocodile winked the other eye, and lifted half his tail out of the mud; and the Elephant's Child stepped back most politely, because he did not wish to be spanked again.

"Come hither, Little One," said the Crocodile. "Why do you ask such things?"

" 'Scuse me," said the Elephant's Child most politely, "but my father has spanked me, my mother has spanked me, not to mention my tall aunt, the Ostrich, and my tall uncle, the Giraffe, who can kick ever so hard, as well as my broad aunt, the Hippopotamus, and my hairy uncle, the Baboon, *and* including the Bi-Coloured-Python-Rock-Snake, with the scalesome, flailsome tail, just up the bank, who spanks harder than any of them; and *so*, if it's quite all the same to you, I don't want to be spanked any more."

"Come hither, Little One," said the Crocodile,

"for I am the Crocodile," and he wept crocodile-tears to show it was quite true.

Then the Elephant's Child grew all breathless, and panted, and kneeled down on the bank and said, "You are the very person I have been looking for all these long days. Will you please tell me what you have for dinner?"

"Come hither, Little One," said the Crocodile, "and I'll whisper."

Then the Elephant's Child put his head down close to the Crocodile's musky, tusky mouth, and the Crocodile caught him by his little nose, which up to that very week, day, hour, and minute, had been no bigger than a boot, though much more useful.

"I think," said the Crocodile—and he said it between his teeth, like this—"I think today I will begin with Elephant's Child!"

At this, O Best Beloved, the Elephant's Child was much annoyed, and he said, speaking through his nose, like this, "Led go! You are hurtig be!"

Then the Bi-Coloured-Python-Rock-Snake scuffled down from the bank and said, "My young friend, if you do not now, immediately and instantly, pull as hard as ever you can, it is my opinion that your acquaintance in the large-pattern

The Elephant's Child

leather ulster" (and by this he meant the Crocodile) "will jerk you into yonder limpid stream before you can say Jack Robinson."

This is the way Bi-Coloured-Python-Rock-Snakes always talk.

Then the Elephant's Child sat back on his little haunches, and pulled, and pulled, and pulled, and his nose began to stretch. And the Crocodile floundered into the water, making it all creamy with great sweeps of his tail, and *he* pulled, and pulled, and pulled.

And the Elephant's Child's nose kept on stretching; and the Elephant's Child spread all his little four legs and pulled, and pulled, and pulled, and his nose kept on stretching; and the Crocodile threshed his tail like an oar, and *he* pulled, and pulled, and pulled, and at each pull the Elephant's Child's nose grew longer and longer—and it hurt him hijjus!

Then the Elephant's Child felt his legs slipping, and he said through his nose, which was now nearly five feet long, "This is too butch for be!"

Then the Bi-Coloured-Python-Rock-Snake came down from the bank, and knotted himself in a double-clove-hitch round the Elephant's Child's hind legs, and said, "Rash and inexperienced traveller, we will now seriously devote ourselves to a little high tension, because if we do not, it is my impression that yonder self-propelling man-of-war with the armour-plated upper deck" (and by this, O Best Beloved, he meant the Crocodile), "will permanently vitiate your future career."

That is the way all Bi-Coloured-Python-Rock-Snakes always talk.

So he pulled, and the Elephant's Child pulled, and the Crocodile pulled; but the Elephant's Child and the Bi-Coloured-Python-Rock-Snake pulled hardest; and at last the Crocodile let go of the Elephant's Child's nose with a plop that you could hear all up and down the Limpopo.

Then the Elephant's Child sat down most hard and sudden; but first he was careful to say "Thank you" to the Bi-Coloured-Python-Rock-Snake; and next he was kind to his poor pulled nose, and wrapped it all up in cool banana leaves, and hung it in the great grey-green, greasy Limpopo to cool.

"What are you doing that for?" said the Bi-Coloured-Python-Rock-Snake.

" 'Scuse me," said the Elephant's Child, "but my nose is badly out of shape, and I am waiting for it to shrink."

"Then you will have to wait a long time," said the Bi-Coloured-Python-Rock-Snake. "Some people do not know what is good for them."

The Elephant's Child sat there for three days

The Elephant's Child

waiting for his nose to shrink. But it never grew any shorter, and, besides, it made him squint. For, O Best Beloved, you will see and understand that the Crocodile had pulled it out into a really truly trunk same as all Elephants have to-day.

At the end of the third day a fly came and stung him on the shoulder, and before he knew what he was doing he lifted up his trunk and hit that fly dead with the end of it.

" 'Vantage number one!" said the Bi-Coloured-Python-Rock-Snake. "You couldn't have done that with a mere-smear nose. Try and eat a little now."

Before he thought what he was doing the Elephant's Child put out his trunk and plucked a large bundle of grass, dusted it clean against his fore-legs, and stuffed it into his own mouth.

" 'Vantage number two!" said the Bi-Coloured-Python-Rock-Snake. "You couldn't have done that with a mere-smear nose. Don't you think the sun is very hot here?"

"It is," said the Elephant's Child; and before he thought what he was doing he schlooped up a schloop of mud from the banks of the great grey-green, greasy Limpopo, and slapped it on his head, where it made a cool schloopy-sloshy mud-cap all trickly behind his ears.

"'Vantage number three!" said the Bi-Coloured-Python-Rock-Snake. "You couldn't have done that with a mere-smear nose. Now how do you feel about being spanked again?"

"'Scuse me," said the Elephant's Child, "but I should not like it at all."

"How would you like to spank somebody?" said the Bi-Coloured-Python-Rock-Snake.

"I should like it very much indeed," said the Elephant's Child.

"Well," said the Bi-Coloured-Python-Rock-Snake, "you will find that new nose of yours very useful to spank people with."

"Thank you," said the Elephant's Child, "I'll remember that; and now I think I'll go home to all my dear families and try."

So the Elephant's Child went home across Africa frisking and whisking his trunk. When he wanted fruit to eat he pulled fruit down from a tree, instead of waiting for it to fall as he used to do. When he wanted grass he plucked grass up from the ground, instead of going on his knees as he used to do. When the flies bit him he broke off the branch of a tree and used it as a fly-whisk; and he made himself a new, cool, slushy-squshy mud-cap whenever the sun was hot. When he felt lonely walking through Africa he sang to himself down his trunk, and the noise was louder than several brass bands. He went especially out of his way to find a broad Hippopotamus (she was no relation of his), and he spanked her very hard, to make sure that the Bi-Coloured-Python-Rock-Snake had spoken the truth about his new trunk. The rest of the time he picked up the melon rinds that he had dropped on his way to the Limpopo—for he was a Tidy Pachyderm.

One dark evening he came back to all his dear families, and he coiled up his trunk and said, "How do you do?" They were very glad to see him, and immediately said, "Come here and be spanked for your 'satiable curtiosity."

"Pooh," said the Elephant's Child. "I don't think you peoples know anything about spanking; but *I* do, and I'll show you."

Then he uncurled his trunk and knocked two of his dear brothers head over heels.

"O Bananas!" said they, "where did you learn that trick, and what have you done to your nose?"

"I got a new one from the Crocodile on the banks of the great grey-green, greasy Limpopo River," said the Elephant's Child. "I asked him what he had for dinner, and he gave me this to keep."

"It looks very ugly," said his hairy uncle, the Baboon.

"It does," said the Elephant's Child. "But it's very useful," and he picked up his hairy uncle, the Baboon, by one hairy leg, and hove him into a hornet's nest.

Then that bad Elephant's Child spanked all his dear families for a long time, till they were very warm and greatly astonished. He pulled out his tall Ostrich aunt's tail-feathers; and he caught his tall uncle, the Giraffe, by the hindleg, and dragged him through a thorn-bush; and he shouted at his broad aunt, the Hippopotamus, and blew bubbles into her ear when she was sleeping in the water after meals; but he never let any one touch Kolokolo Bird.

At last things grew so exciting that his dear families went off one by one in a hurry to the banks of the great-grey-green, greasy Limpopo River, all set about with fever-trees, to borrow new noses from the Crocodile. When they came back nobody spanked anybody any more; and ever since that day, O Best Beloved, all the Elephants you will ever see, besides all those that you won't, have trunks precisely like the trunk of the 'satiable Elephant's Child.

I keep six honest serving-men;
    (They taught me all I knew)
Their names are What and Why and When

And How and Where and Who.
I send them over land and sea,
   I send them east and west;
But after they have worked for me,
   I give them all a rest.

I let them rest from nine till five,
   For I am busy then,
As well as breakfast, lunch, and tea,
   For they are hungry men:
But different folk have different views,
   I know a person small—
She keeps ten million serving-men,
   Who get no rest at all!

She sends 'em abroad on her own affairs,
   From the second she opens her eyes—
One million Hows, two million Wheres,
   And seven million Whys!

THE MESSENGER TO MAFTAM

AMONG the Soninke people, many days on foot north of the Gulf of Guinea, there lived a man by the name of Mamadi. He was poor, and lived in a small and unpretentious house. Yet Mamadi was much respected everywhere because it was said that he never told a falsehood, no matter how small.

One day Bahene, chief of the Soninke, after having heard a long conversation about Mamadi, said in an irritated way:

"Who is this man Mamadi who is so full of virtue and cleverness that he never makes a false statement?"

"He lives in the small village of Ogo," his councilors told him. "He is known far and wide, because he never says a thing that isn't so."

"I believe this character is an exaggeration," the chief said. "There is no such man, either in the desert or the plains. Have him brought here for me to see."

The Messenger to Maftam

So the messengers brought Mamadi to the chief, and Bahene said to him:

"Mamadi, is it true that you have never lied?"

"Yes, it is true," Mamadi said.

"It is hard to believe," Bahene said. "There is no one alive who hasn't at some time or other said something that wasn't strictly so. Yet, the people say it is true. But tell me, are you certain that you won't ever tell an untruth?"

"Yes, I am quite certain," Mamadi answered.

"How can one be so sure of such a thing?" Bahene asked. "Isn't it presumptuous to say in advance what one will do, without even considering the circumstances?"

"The circumstances are quite unimportant," Mamadi said, "for I am unable to say what is false."

"Well, you seem to be a virtuous man," Bahene said. "If your tongue is as faithful to your principles as you say, then I'm wrong in thinking there is no man who doesn't lie. But if you do lie, then you will commit an act more offensive than when an ordinary person lies, because the ordinary person makes no such virtue of his tongue. So take care, Mamadi, for the day you do tell a lie will be a bad one for you. If the

Soninke people ever catch you in a falsehood, I'll have you beaten with ropes!"

When Mamadi had gone back to his village, Bahene said to his councilors:

"That village man is putting on airs! He must have some virtue, since his reputation is widespread. But it requires more than virtue to tell no falsehoods, it takes cleverness as well. Mamadi's certainty that he can't tell a lie is arrogant. He needs a lesson!"

Early one morning, several days later, Bahene sent for Mamadi again. The village man arrived before Bahene's house to find him and his men standing with their weapons in their hands.

"Mamadi, I need you to do a service for me. Please go to my other house in the village of Maftam to deliver a message to my wife. Tell her that we have gone hunting for antelope, and that we shall arrive at Maftam today at noon. We shall be very hungry and shall want plenty to eat. Wait there, and you will eat with us."

Bahene and his hunters started out as though to hunt, while Mamadi took the trail to Maftam, hurrying so that he would get the message there in time for the chief's wife to prepare food. But as soon as Mamadi was out of sight, Bahene turned around and went back to his house. He put down his weapons, and said to the men in his hunting party:

"Well, I have changed my mind! We won't go hunting after all. Nor will we go to Maftam today. This country fellow Mamadi who carries the message to my wife believes that he can't tell an untruth. We'll see. He will tell my wife that we are hunting and that we are going to bring an antelope. He will tell her that we shall arrive at noon, and that we will be very hungry. But none of these things will happen. When we finally get there we shall have a great laugh, for the poor villager's wisdom isn't as great as his virtue. And then Mamadi shall be beaten for his arrogance."

Mamadi hurried to Maftam. It was three hours away on foot. When he arrived he went to Bahene's wife and said to her:

"I am carrying an urgent message from Bahene."

"What is it?" she asked him.

"Of that I am not sure," Mamadi said.

"How can you carry a message of which you aren't sure?"

Bahene's wife was getting angry.

"What are you supposed to tell me?"

"It is likely, rather, or so it seemed, perhaps,

possibly, or, on the other hand more or less certainly, probably less than more, or more than less, that Bahene went hunting."

"It's not very clear," Bahene's wife said. "Did he or didn't he?"

"It's the way I said," Mamadi went on. "When I saw him and the hunters they were clearly going hunting. I could tell by the way they stood around with their weapons in their hands. Yet of course people sometimes stand around like that when they have just returned from the hunt. It's not likely that they just returned from the hunt, though, because there wasn't any meat, but of course they could have hunted and not found any game, so I suppose they were going hunting instead of coming back, more or less, to be sure, somewhat, none the less, however, or at least that was the general impression that was to be gained from the conversation, which was fairly explicit, in a way . . ."

"Try not to get excited," Bahene's wife said. "I don't yet understand whether he is going hunting or not. But what other news is there?"

"Well, it would be wise to be prepared to cook an antelope, of some sort, just about, in case they catch one, although certainly that is Bahene's general intention, possibly, most likely, more or less, that is, in the event they have gone hunting."

"Of all the people among the Soninke villages, Bahene had to pick you!" she said in disgust. "What else is there to know, almost?"

"Oh, yes, there won't be much time, it would seem, and Bahene's hunting party will assuredly, in all likelihood, be somewhat, or exceedingly, or conceivably hardly at all, hungry, when they arrive here exactly or approximately at noon, if they do, although it is most probable, and there is no grave doubt that they won't, even though some question arises as to the certainty, of which there could be some doubt, within bounds, probably . . ."

"Wait! Stop a moment!" Bahene's wife cried out. "So far I haven't learned a thing! Is there something more precise you can tell me?"

"Something more?" Mamadi continued. "Oh, yes. I am to wait for him here until he arrives, if that is possible, or even likely, or otherwise . . ."

"Stop your babbling!" Bahene's wife said. "Is he coming or isn't he? And when will he be here?"

"Well, now, as I said before, more or less clearly than I might have, somewhat, or not altogether, it appears, seemingly, though not conclusively, or even assuredly, that Bahene might, at least ought to, sooner or later . . ."

"Never mind!" Bahene's wife interrupted. "Tell me no more! The more you say the less I know!"

Then Mamadi lay down upon a mat to await the chief's arrival. Noon came and went, but Bahene and his hunters didn't appear. Night came, then morning, and finally the chief arrived in Maftam with his following. They all laughed as they saw their messenger waiting for them in the court.

"Well, our meal is perhaps a little spoiled, but no matter," Bahene said, "for we have proved that even a most virtuous man may allow his tongue to speak a lie, and that this man's arrogance is more noteworthy than his virtues."

"How is that?" Bahene's wife asked.

"Why, he told you that we had gone hunting, when we hadn't, and that we would be here yesterday noon, when we weren't, and that we would bring an antelope, which we didn't. So now he is to be beaten as a lesson to him."

"No," the chief's wife said, "he said that you would do this or you wouldn't, that it was likely or unlikely, or certain or uncertain. He delivered the message, but he gave it with so many qualifications and exceptions that I really didn't get any sense out of him at all."

Bahene was crestfallen. It was he, not Mamadi, who was shamed in public. So he had presents given to Mamadi, and said to him:

"I was wrong, Mamadi, and you are, in truth, a virtuous and wise man. I know now what all the other Soninke people already knew, that you will never tell a lie."

"That is quite true," Mamadi replied. "I never never shall, presumably, it is certain, probably . . ."

THE COW-TAIL SWITCH

NEAR THE EDGE of the Liberian rain forest, on a hill overlooking the Cavally River, was the village of Kundi. Its rice and cassava fields spread in all directions. Cattle grazed in the grassland near the river. Smoke from the fires in the round clay houses seeped through the palmleaf roofs, and from a distance these faint columns of smoke seemed to hover over the village. Men and boys fished in the river with nets, and women pounded grain in wooden mortars before the houses.

In this village, with his wife and many children, lived a hunter by the name of Ogaloussa.

One morning Ogaloussa took his weapons down from the wall of his house and went into the forest to hunt. His wife and his children went to tend their fields, and drove their cattle out to graze. The day passed, and they ate their evening meal of manioc and fish. Darkness came, but Ogaloussa didn't return.

Another day went by, and still Ogaloussa didn't come back. They talked about it and wondered what could have detained him. A week passed, then a month. Sometimes Ogaloussa's sons mentioned that he hadn't come home. The family cared for the crops, and the sons hunted for game, but after a while they no longer talked about Ogaloussa's disappearance.

Then, one day, another son was born to Ogaloussa's wife. His name was Puli. Puli grew older. He began to sit up and crawl. The time came when Puli began to talk, and the first thing he said was, "Where is my father?"

The other sons looked across the ricefields.

"Yes," one of them said. "Where is Father?"

"He should have returned long ago," another one said.

"Something must have happened. We ought to look for him," a third son said.

"He went into the forest, but where will we find him?" another one asked.

"I saw him go," one of them said. "He went that way, across the river. Let us follow the trail and search for him."

So the sons took their weapons and started out to look for Ogaloussa. When they were deep among the great trees and vines of the forest they lost the trail. They searched in the forest until one of them found the trail again. They followed it until they lost the way once more, and then another son found the trail. It was dark in the forest, and many times they became lost. Each time another son found the way. At last they came to a clearing among the trees, and there on the ground scattered about lay Ogaloussa's bones and his rusted weapons. They knew then that Ogaloussa had been killed in the hunt.

One of the sons stepped forward and said, "I know how to put a dead person's bones together." He gathered all of Ogaloussa's bones and put them together, each in its right place.

Another son said, "I have knowledge too. I know how to cover the skeleton with sinews and flesh." He went to work, and he covered Ogaloussa's bones with sinews and flesh.

A third son said, "I have the power to put blood into a body." He went forward and put blood into Ogaloussa's veins, and then he stepped aside.

Another of the sons said, "I can put breath into a body." He did his work, and when he was through they saw Ogaloussa's chest rise and fall.

"I can give the power of movement to a body," another of them said. He put the power of movement into his father's body, and Ogaloussa sat up and opened his eyes.

"I can give him the power of speech," another son said. He gave the body the power of speech, and then he stepped back.

Ogaloussa looked around him. He stood up.

"Where are my weapons?" he asked.

They picked up his rusted weapons from the grass where they lay and gave them to him. They then returned the way they had come, through the forest and the ricefields, until they had arrived once more in the village.

Ogaloussa went into his house. His wife prepared a bath for him and he bathed. She prepared food for him and he ate. Four days he remained in the house, and on the fifth day he came out and shaved his head, because this was what people did when they came back from the land of the dead.

Afterwards he killed a cow for a great feast. He took the cow's tail and braided it. He decorated it with beads and cowry shells and bits of shiny metal. It was a beautiful thing. Ogaloussa carried it with him to important affairs. When there was a dance or an important ceremony he always had it with him. The people of the village thought it was the most beautiful cow-tail switch they had ever seen.

Soon there was a celebration in the village because Ogaloussa had returned from the dead. The people dressed in their best clothes, the musicians brought out their instruments, and a big dance began. The drummers beat their drums and the women sang. The people drank much palm wine. Everyone was happy.

Ogaloussa carried his cow-tail switch, and everyone admired it. Some of the men grew bold and came forward to Ogaloussa and asked for the cow-tail switch, but Ogaloussa kept it in his hand. Now and then there was a clamor and much confusion as many people asked for it at once. The women and children begged for it too, but Ogaloussa refused them all.

Finally he stood up to talk. The dancing stopped and people came close to hear what Ogaloussa had to say.

"A long time ago I went into the forest," Ogaloussa said. "While I was hunting I was killed by a leopard. Then my sons came for me. They brought me back from the land of the dead to my village. I will give this cow-tail switch to one of my sons. All of them have done something to bring me back from the dead, but I have only one cow tail to give. I shall give it to the one who did the most to bring me home."

So an argument started.

The Cow-Tail Switch

"He will give it to me!" one of the sons said. "It was I who did the most, for I found the trail in the forest when it was lost!"

"No, he will give it to me!" another son said. "It was I who put his bones together!"

"It was I who covered his bones with sinews and flesh!" another said. "He will give it to me!"

"It was I who gave him the power of movement!" another son said. "I deserve it most!"

Another son said it was he who should have the switch, because he had put blood in Ogaloussa's veins. Another claimed it because he had put breath in the body. Each of the sons argued his right to possess the wonderful cow-tail switch.

Before long not only the sons but the other people of the village were talking. Some of them argued that the son who had put blood in Ogaloussa's veins should get the switch, others that the one who had given Ogaloussa's breath should get it. Some of them believed that all of the sons had done equal things, and that they should share it. They argued back and forth this way until Ogaloussa asked them to be quiet.

"To this son I will give the cow-tail switch, for I owe most to him," Ogaloussa said.

He came forward and bent low and handed it

to Puli, the little boy who had been born while Ogaloussa was in the forest.

The people of the village remembered then that the child's first words had been, "Where is my father?" They knew that Ogaloussa was right.

For it was a saying among them that a man is not really dead until he is forgotten.

AESOP'S FABLES

THE BAT, THE BIRDS, AND THE BEASTS

A great conflict was about to come off between the Birds and Beasts. When the two armies were collected together the Bat hesitated which to join. The Birds that passed his perch said: "Come with us;" but he said: "I am a beast." Later on, some Beasts who were passing underneath him looked up and said: "Come with us"; but he said: "I am a Bird." Luckily at the last moment peace was made, and no battle took place, so the Bat came to the Birds and wished to join in the rejoicings, but they all turned against him and he had to fly away. He then went to the Beasts, but soon had to beat a retreat, or else they would have torn him to pieces, "Ah," said the Bat, "I see now
"He That Is neither One Thing nor the Other Has No Friends."

THE HARE WITH MANY FRIENDS

A Hare was very popular with the other beasts who all claimed to be her friends. But one day she heard the hounds approaching and hoped to escape them by the aid of her many Friends. So she went to the horse, and asked him to carry her away from the hounds on his back. But he declined, stating that he had important work to do for his master. He felt sure, he said, that all her other friends would come to her assistance. She then applied to the bull, and hoped that he would repel the hounds with his horns. The bull replied: "I am very sorry, but I have an appointment with a lady; but I feel sure that our friend the goat will do what you want." The goat, however, feared that his back might do her some harm if he took her upon it. The ram, he felt sure, was the proper friend to apply to. So she went to the ram and told him the case. The ram replied: "Another time, my dear friend, I do not like to interfere on the present occasion, as hounds have been known to eat sheep as well as hares." The Hare then applied, as a last hope, to the calf, who regretted that he was unable to help her, as he did not like to take the responsibility upon himself, as so many older

persons than himself had declined the task. By this time the hounds were quite near and the Hare took to her heels and luckily escaped.
"He That Has Many Friends, Has No Friends"

THE LION AND THE STATUE

A Man and a Lion were discussing the relative strength of men and lions in general. The Man contended that he and his fellows were stronger than lions by reason of the greater intelligence. "Come now with me," he cried "and I will soon prove that I am right." So he took him into the public gardens and showed him a statue of Hercules overcoming the Lion and tearing his mouth in two.

"That is all very well," said the Lion, "but proves nothing, for it was a man who made the statue,"
"We Can Easily Represent Things as We Wish Them to Be."

THE BUFFOON AND THE COUNTRYMAN

At a county fair there was a Buffoon who made all the people laugh by imitating the cries of various animals. He finished off by speaking so like a pig that the spectators thought that he had a porker concealed about him. But a Countryman who stood by said: "Call that a pig's squeak! Nothing like it. You give me till tomorrow and I will show you what it's like." The audience laughed, but next day, sure enough, the Countryman appeared on the stage, and putting his head down squealed so hideously that the spectators hissed and threw stones at him to make him stop. "You fools!" he cried, "see what you have been hissing," and held up a little pig whose ear he had been pinching to make him utter the squeals.

*"Men Often Applaud an Imitation and
Hiss the Real Thing."*

THE ASS'S BRAINS

The Lion and the Fox went hunting together. The Lion, on the advice of the Fox, sent a message to the Ass, proposing to make an alliance between their two families. The Ass came to the place of meeting, overjoyed at the prospect of a royal alliance. But when he came there the Lion simply pounced on the Ass, and said to the Fox: "Here is our dinner for to-day. Watch you here while I go and have a nap. Woe betide you if you touch my prey." The Lion went away and the Fox waited; but finding that his master did not return, ventured to take out the brains of the Ass and ate them up. When the Lion came back he soon noticed the absence of the brains, and asked the Fox in a terrible voice: "What have you done with the brains?"

"Brains, your Majesty! it had none, or it would never have fallen into your trap."

"Wit Has Always an Answer Ready."

THE FOX, THE COCK, AND THE DOG

On moonlight night a Fox was prowling about a farmer's hencoop, and saw a Cock roosting high up beyond his reach. "Good news, good news! he cried.

"Why, what is that?" said the Cock.

"King Lion has declared a universal truce. No beast may hurt a bird henceforth but all shall dwell together in brotherly friendship."

"Why, that is good news," said the Cock; "and there I see some one coming, with whom we can share the good tidings." And so saying he craned his neck forward and looked afar off.

"What is it you see?" said the Fox.

"It is only my master's Dog that is coming

toward us. What, going so soon?" he continued, as the Fox began to turn away as soon as he had heard the news. "Will you not stop and congratulate the Dog on the reign of universal peace?"

"I would gladly do so," said the Fox, "but I fear he may not have heard of King Lion's decree."

"Cunning Often Outwits Itself."

THE TRUMPETER TAKEN PRISONER

A trumpeter during a battle ventured too near the enemy and was captured by them. They were about to proceed to put him to death when he begged them to hear his plea for mercy. "I do not fight," said he, "and indeed carry no weapon; I only blow this trumpet, and surely that cannot harm you; then why should you kill me?"

"You may not fight yourself," said the others, "but you encourage and guide your men to the fight."

"Words May Be Deeds."

THE TOWN MOUSE AND THE COUNTRY MOUSE

Now you must know that a Town Mouse once upon a time went on a visit to his cousin in the country. He was rough and ready, this cousin, but he loved his town friend and made him heartily welcome. Beans and bacon, cheese and bread, were all he had to offer, but he offered them freely. The Town Mouse rather turned up his long nose at this country fare, and said: "I cannot understand, Cousin, how you can put up with such poor food as this, but of course you cannot expect anything better in the country; come you with me and I will show you how to live. When you have been in town a week you will wonder how you could ever have stood a country life." No sooner said than done: the two mice set off for the town and arrived at the Town Mouse's residence late at night. "You will want some refreshment after our long journey," said the polite Town Mouse, and took his friend into the grand dining-room. There they found the remains of a fine feast, and soon the two mice were eating up jellies and cakes and all that was nice. Suddenly they heard growling and barking. "What is that? said the Country

Mouse. "It is only the dogs of the house," answered the other. "Only!" said the Country Mouse. "I do not like that music at my dinner." Just at that moment the door flew open, in came two huge mastiffs, and the two mice had to scamper down and run off. "Good-bye, Cousin," said the Country Mouse. "What! go so soon?" said the other. "Yes," he replied:

*"Better Beans and Bacon in Peace than
Cakes and Ale in Fear."*

THE DOG AND THE WOLF

A gaunt Wolf was almost dead with hunger when he happened to meet a House-dog who was passing by. "Ah, Cousin," said the Dog, "I knew how it would be; your irregular life will soon be the ruin of you. Why do you not work steadily as I do, and get your food regularly given to you?"

"I would have no objection," said the Wolf, "if I could only get a place."

"I will easily arrange that for you," said the Dog; "come with me to my master and you shall share my work."

So the Wolf and the Dog went towards the town together. On the way there the Wolf noticed that the hair on a certain part of the Dog's neck was very much worn away, so he asked him how that had come about.

"Oh, it is nothing," said the Dog. "That is only the place where the collar is put on at night to keep me chained up; it chafes a bit, but one soon gets used to it."

"Is that all?" said the Wolf. "Then good-bye to you, Master Dog."

"Better Starve Free than Be a Fat Slave."

THE HORSE AND THE ASS

A Horse and an Ass were traveling together, the Horse prancing along in its fine trappings, the Ass carrying with difficulty the heavy weight in its panniers. "I wish I were you," sighed the Ass; "nothing to do and well fed, and all that fine harness upon you." Next day, however, there was a great battle, and the Horse was wounded to death in the final charge of the day. His friend, the Ass, happened to pass by shortly afterwards and found him on the point of death. "I was wrong," said the Ass:
"Better Humble Security than Gilded Danger."

THE FOX AND THE STORK

At one time the Fox and the Stork were on visiting terms and seemed very good friends. So the Fox invited the Stork to dinner, and for a joke put nothing before her but some soup in a very shallow dish. This the Fox could easily lap up, but the Stork could only wet the end of her long bill in it, and left the meal as hungry as when she began. "I am sorry," said the Fox, "the soup is not to your liking."

"Pray do not apologise," said the Stork. "I hope you will return this visit, and come and dine with me soon." So a day was appointed when the Fox should visit the Stork; but when they were seated at table all that was for their dinner was contained in a very long-necked jar with a narrow mouth, in which the Fox could not insert his snout, so all he could manage to do was to lick the outside of the jar.

"I will not apologise for the dinner," said the Stork:

"One Bad Turn Deserves Another."

THE OLD MAN AND DEATH

An old labourer, bent double with age and toil, was gathering sticks in a forest. At last he grew so tired and hopeless that he threw down the bundle of sticks, and cried out: "I cannot bear this life any longer. Ah, I wish Death would only come and take me!"

As he spoke, Death, a grisly skeleton, appeared and said to him: "What wouldst thou, Mortal? I heard thee call me."

"Please, sir," replied the woodcutter, "would you kindly help me to lift this faggot of sticks on to my shoulder?"

"We Would Often Be Sorry if Our Wishes Were Gratified."

THE TWO CRABS

One fine day two Crabs came out from their home to take a stroll on the sand. "Child," said the mother, "you are walking very ungracefully. You should accustom yourself to walking straight forward without twisting from side to side."

"Pray, mother," said the young one, "do but set the example yourself, and I will follow you."

"Example Is the Best Precept."

THE YOUNG THIEF AND HIS MOTHER

A young Man had been caught in a daring act of theft and had been condemned to be executed for it. He expressed his desire to see his Mother, and to speak with her before he was led to execution, and of course this was granted. When his Mother came to him he said: "I want to whisper to you," and when she brought her ear near him, he nearly bit it off. All the bystanders were horrified, and asked him what he could mean by such brutal and inhuman conduct. "It is to punish her," he said. "When I was young I began with stealing little things, and brought them home to Mother. Instead of rebuking and punishing me, she laughed and said: 'It will not be noticed.' It is because of her that I am here to-day."

"He is right, woman," said the Priest; "the Lord hath said:
"Train up a Child in the Way He Should Go; and When He Is Old He Will Not Depart Therefrom."

THE MAN, THE BOY, AND THE DONKEY

A man and his son were once going with their Donkey to market. As they were walking along by its side a countryman passed them and said: "You fools, what is a Donkey for but to ride upon?"

So the Man put the Boy on the Donkey and they went on their way. But soon they passed a group of men, one of whom said: "See that lazy youngster, he lets his father walk while he rides."

So the Man ordered his Boy to get off, and got on himself. But they hadn't gone far when they passed two women, one of whom said to the other: "Shame on that lazy lout to let his poor little son trudge along."

Well, the Man didn't know what to do, but at last he took his Boy up before him on the Donkey. By this time they had come to the town, and the passers-by began to jeer and point at them. The Man stopped and asked what they were scoffing at. The men said: "Aren't you ashamed of yourself for overloading that poor Donkey of yours—you and your hulking son?"

The Man and Boy got off and tried to think what to do. They thought and they thought, till at last they cut down a pole, tied the Donkey's feet to it and raised the pole and the Donkey to their shoulders. They went along amid the laughter of all who met them till they came to

Market Bridge, when the Donkey, getting one of his feet loose, kicked out and caused the Boy to drop his end of the pole. In the struggle the Donkey fell over the bridge, and his forefeet being tied together he was drowned.

"That will teach you," said an old man who had followed them:

"Please All, and You Will Please None."

THE FROG AND THE OX

"Oh Father," said a little Frog to the big one sitting by the side of a pool, "I have seen such a terrible monster! It was as big as a mountain, with horns on its head, and a long tail, and it had hoofs divided in two."

"Tush, child, tush," said the old Frog, "that was only Farmer White's Ox. It isn't so big either; he may be a little bit taller than I, but I could easily make myself quite as broad; just you see." So he blew himself out, and blew himself out, and blew himself out. "Was he as big as that?" asked he.

"Oh, much bigger than that," said the young Frog.

Again the old one blew himself out, and asked the young one if the Ox was as big as that.

"Bigger, father, bigger," was the reply.

So the Frog took a deep breath, and blew and blew and blew, and swelled and swelled and swelled. And then he said: "I'm sure the Ox is not as big as—" But at this moment he burst.
"*Self-Conceit May Lead to Self-Destruction.*"

THE EAGLE AND THE ARROW

An Eagle was soaring through the air when suddenly it heard the whiz of an Arrow, and felt itself wounded to death. Slowly it fluttered down to the earth, with its lifeblood pouring out of it. Looking down upon the Arrow with which it had been pierced, it found that the shaft of the Arrow had been feathered with one of its own plumes. "Alas!" it cried, as it died,
"*We Often Give Our Enemies the Means
for Our own Destruction.*"

THE SWALLOW AND THE OTHER BIRDS

It happened that a Countryman was sowing some hemp seeds in a field where a Swallow and some other birds were hopping about picking up their food. "Beware of that man," quoth the

Swallow. "Why, what is he doing?" said the others. "That is hemp seed he is sowing; be careful to pick up every one of the seeds, or else you will repent it." The birds paid no heed to the Swallow's words, and by and by the hemp grew up and was made into cord, and of the cords nets were made, and many a bird that had despised the Swallow's advice was caught in nets made out of that very hemp. "What did I tell you?" said the Swallow.

"Destroy the Seed of Evil, or It Will Grow Up to Your Ruin."

THE MOTH AND THE STAR

A young and impressionable moth once set his heart on a certain star. He told his mother about this and she counselled him to set his heart on a bridge lamp instead. "Stars aren't the thing to hang around," she said; "lamps are the thing to hang around." "You get somewhere that way," said the moth's father. "You don't get anywhere chasing stars." But the moth would not heed the words of either parent. Every evening at dusk when the star came out he would start flying toward it and every morning at dawn he would crawl back home worn out with his vain endeavor. One day his father said to him, "You have't burned a wing in months, boy, and it looks to me as if you were never going to. All your brothers have been badly burned flying around street lamps and all your sisters have been terribly singed flying around house lamps. Come on, now, get out of here and get yourself scorched! A big strapping moth like you without a mark on him!"

The moth left his father's house, but he would not fly around street lamps and he would not fly around house lamps. He went right on trying to reach the star, which was four and one-third light years, or twenty-five trillion miles, away. The moth thought it was just caught in the top branches of an elm. He never did reach the star, but he went right on trying, night after night, and when he was a very, very old moth he began to think that he really had reached the star and he went around saying so. This gave him a deep and lasting pleasure, and he lived to a great old age. His parents and his brothers and his sisters had all been burned to death when they were quite young.

Moral: Who flies afar from the sphere of our sorrow is here today and here tomorrow.

THE OWL WHO WAS GOD

Once upon a starless midnight there was an owl who sat on the branch of an oak tree. Two ground moles tried to slip quietly by, unnoticed. "You!" said the owl. "Who?" they quavered, in fear and astonishment, for they could not believe it was possible for anyone to see them in that thick darkness. "You two!" said the owl. The moles hurried away and told the other creatures of the field and forest that the owl was the greatest and wisest of all animals because he could see in the dark and because he could answer any question. "I'll see about that," said a secretary bird, and he called on the owl one night when it was again very dark. "How many claws am I holding up?" said the secretary bird. "Two," said the owl, and that was right. "Can you give me another expression for 'that is to say' or 'namely'?" asked the secretary bird. "To wit," said the owl. "Why does a lover call on his love?" asked the secretary bird. "To woo," said the owl.

The secretary bird hastened back to the other creatures and reported that the owl was indeed the greatest and wisest animal in the world because he could see in the dark and because he could answer any question. "Can he see in the daytime, too?" asked a red fox. "Yes," echoed a dormouse and a French poodle. "Can he see in the daytime, too?" All the other creatures laughed loudly at this silly question, and they set upon the red fox and his friends and drove them out of the region. Then they sent a messenger to the owl and asked him to be their leader.

When the owl appeared among the animals it was high noon and the sun was shining brightly. He walked very slowly, which gave him an appearance of great dignity, and he peered about him with large, staring eyes, which gave him an air of tremendous importance. "He's God!" screamed a Plymouth Rock hen. and the others took up the cry "He's God!" So they followed him wherever he went and when he began to bump into things they began to bump into things, too. Finally he came to a concrete highway and he started up the middle of it and all the other creatures followed him. Presently a hawk, who was acting as outrider, observed a truck coming toward them at fifty miles an hour, and he reported to the secretary bird and the secretary bird reported to the owl. "There's danger ahead," said the secretary bird. "To wit?" said the owl. The secretary bird told him. "Aren't you afraid?" he asked. "Who?" said the owl calmly, for he could not see the truck. "He's God!" cried all the creatures again, and they were still crying "He's God!" when the truck hit them and ran them down. Some of the animals were merely injured, but most of them, including the owl, were killed.

Moral: You can fool too many of the people too much of the time.

THE UNICORN IN THE GARDEN

Once upon a sunny morning a man who sat in a breakfast nook looked up from his scrambled eggs to see a white unicorn with a golden horn quietly cropping the roses in the garden. The man went up to the bedroom where his wife was still asleep and woke her. "There's a unicorn in the garden," he said. "Eating roses." She opened one unfriendly eye and looked at him. "The unicorn is a mythical beast," she said, and turned her back on him. The man walked slowly downstairs and out into the garden. The unicorn was still there; he was now browsing among the tulips. "Here, unicorn," said the man and he pulled up a lily and gave it to him. The unicorn ate it gravely. With a high heart, because there was a unicorn in his garden, the man went upstairs and roused his wife again. "The unicorn, he said, "ate a lily." He wife sat up in bed and looked at him, coldly. "You are a booby," she said, "and I am going to have you put in the booby-hatch." The man, who had never like the words "booby" and "booby hatch," and who liked them even less on a shining morning when there was a unicorn in the the garden, thought for a moment. "We'll see about that," he said.

He walked over to the door. "He has a golden horn in the middle of his forehead," he told her. Then he went back to the garden to watch the unicorn; but the unicorn had gone away. The man sat down among the roses and went to sleep.

As soon as the husband had gone out of the house, the wife got up and dressed as fast as she could. She was very excited and there was a gloat in her eye. She telephoned the police and she telephoned a psychiatrist; she told them to hurry to her house and bring a strait-jacket. When the police and the psychiatrist arrived they sat down in chairs and looked at her, with great interest. "My husband," she said, "saw a unicorn this morning." The police looked at the psychiatrist and the psychiatrist looked at the police. "He told me it ate a lily," she said. The psychiatrist looked at the police and the police looked at the psychiatrist. "He told me it had a golden horn in the middle of its forehead," she said. At a solemn signal from the psychiatrist, the police leaped from their chairs and seized the wife. They had a hard time subduing her, for she put up a terrific struggle, but they finally subdued her. Just as they got her into the strait-jacket, the husband came back into the house.

"Did you tell your wife you saw a unicorn?" asked the police. "Of course not," said the husband. "The unicorn is a mythical beast." "That's all I wanted to know," said the psychiatrist. "Take her away. I'm sorry, sir, but your wife is as crazy as a jay bird." So they took her away, cursing and screaming, and shut her up in an institution. The husband lived happily ever after.

Moral: Don't count your boobies until they are hatched.

THE RABBITS WHO CAUSED ALL THE TROUBLE

Within the memory of the youngest child there was a family of rabbits who lived near a pack of wolves. The wolves announced that they did not like the way the rabbits were living. (The wolves were crazy about the way they themselves were living, because it was the only way to live.) One night several wolves were killed in an earthquake and this was blamed on the rabbits, for it is well known that rabbits pound on the ground with their hind legs and cause earthquakes. On another night one of the wolves was killed by a bolt of lightning and this was also blamed on the rabbits, for it is well known that lettuce-eaters cause lightning. The wolves threatened to civilize the rabbits if they didn't behave, and the rabbits decided to run away to a desert island. But the other animals, who lived at a great distance, shamed them, saying, "You must stay where you are and be brave. This is no world for escapists. If the wolves attack you, we will come to your aid, in all probability." So the rabbits continued to live near the wolves and one day there was a terrible flood which drowned a great many wolves. This was blamed on the rabbits, for it is well known that carrot-nibblers with long ears cause floods. The wolves descended on the rabbits, for their own good, and imprisoned them in a dark cave, for their own protection.

When nothing was heard about the rabbits for some weeks, the other animals demanded to know what had happened to them. The wolves replied that the rabbits had been eaten and since they had been eaten the affair was a purely internal matter. But the other animals warned that they might possibly unite against the wolves unless some reason was given for the destruction of the rabbits. So the wolves gave them one. "They were trying to escape," said the wolves, "and, as you know, this is no world for escapists."

Moral: Run, don't walk, to the nearest desert island.

THE STORY OF DOCTOR DOLITTLE

THE FIRST CHAPTER

Puddleby

ONCE UPON A TIME, many years ago—when our grandfathers were little children—there was a doctor; and his name was Dolittle—John Dolittle, M.D. "M.D." means that he was a proper doctor and knew a whole lot.

He lived in a little town called, Puddleby-on-the-Marsh. All the folks, young and old, knew him well by sight. And whenever he walked down the street in his high hat everyone would say, "There goes the Doctor!—He's a clever man." And the dogs and the children would all run up and follow behind him; and even the crows that lived in the church-tower would caw and nod their heads.

The house he lived in, on the edge of the town, was quite small; but his garden was very large and had a wide lawn and stone seats and weeping-willows hanging over. His sister, Sarah Dolittle, was housekeeper for him; but the Doctor looked after the garden himself.

He was very fond of animals and kept many kinds of pets. Besides the gold-fish in the pond at the bottom of his garden, he had rabbits in the pantry, white mice in his piano, a squirrel in the linen closet and a hedgehog in the cellar. He had a cow with a calf too, and an old lame horse—twenty-five years of age—and chickens, and pigeons, and two lambs, and many other animals. But his favorite pets were Dab-Dab the duck, Jip the dog, Gub-Gub the baby pig, Polynesia the parrot, and the owl Too-Too.

His sister used to grumble about all these animals and said they made the house untidy. And one day when an old lady with rheumatism came to see the Doctor, she sat on the hedgehog who was sleeping on the sofa and never came to see him any more, but drove every Saturday all the way to Oxenthorpe, another town ten miles off, to see a different doctor.

Then his sister, Sarah Dolittle, came to him and said,

"John, how can you expect sick people to come and see you when you keep all these animals in the house? It's a fine doctor would have his parlor full of hedgehogs and mice! That's the fourth personage these animals have driven away. Squire Jenkins and the Parson say they wouldn't come near your house again—no matter how sick they are. We are getting poorer every day. If you go on like this, none of the best people will have you for a doctor."

"But I like the animals better than the 'best people'," said the Doctor.

"You are ridiculous," said his sister, and walked out of the room.

So, as time went on, the Doctor got more and more animals; and the people who came to see him got less and less. Till at last he had no one left—except the Cat's-meat-Man, who didn't mind any kind of animals. But the Cat's-meat-Man wasn't very rich and he only got sick once a year—at Christmas-time, when he used to give the Doctor sixpence for a bottle of medicine.

Sixpence a year wasn't enough to live on—even in those days, long ago; and if the Doctor hadn't had some money saved up in his money-box, no one knows what would have happened.

And he kept on getting still more pets; and of course it cost a lot to feed them. And the money he had saved up grew littler and littler.

Then he sold his piano, and let the mice live in a bureau-drawer. But the money he got for that too began to go, so he sold the brown suit he wore on Sundays and went on becoming poorer and poorer.

And now, when he walked down the street in his

high hat, people would say to one another, "There goes John Dolittle, M.D.! There was a time when he was the best known doctor in the West Country —Look at him now—He hasn't any money and his stockings are full of holes!"

But the dogs and the cats and the chidren still ran up and followed him through the town—the same as they had done when he was rich.

THE SECOND CHAPTER

Animal Language

IT HAPPENED ONE DAY that the Doctor was sitting in his kitchen talking with the Cat's-meat-Man who had come to see him with a stomach-ache.

"Why don't you give up being a people's doctor, and be an animal-doctor?" asked the Cat's-meat-Man.

The parrot, Polynesia, was sitting in the window looking out at the rain and singing a sailor-song to herself. She stopped singing and started to listen.

"You see, Doctor," the Cat's-meat-Man went on, "you know all about animals—much more than what these here vets do. That book you wrote—about cats, why, it's wonderful! I can't read or write myself—or maybe *I'd* write some books. But my wife, Theodosia, she's a scholar, she is. And she read your book to me. Well, it's wonderful—that's all can be said—wonderful. You might have been a cat yourself. You know the way they think. And listen: you can make a lot of money doctoring animals. Do you know that? You see, I'd send all the old women who had sick cats or dogs to you. And if they didn't get sick fast enough, I could put something in the meat I sell 'em to make 'em sick, see?"

"Oh, no," said the Doctor quickly. "You mustn't do that. That wouldn't be right."

"Oh, I didn't mean real sick," answered the Cat's-meat-Man. "Just a little something to make them droopy-like was what I had reference to. But as you say, maybe it ain't quite fair on the animals. But they'll get sick anyway, because the old women always give 'em too much to eat. And look, all the farmers 'round about who had lame horses and weak lambs—they'd come. Be an animal-doctor."

When the Cat's-meat-Man had gone the parrot flew off the window on to the Doctor's table and said,

"That man's got sense. That's what you ought to do. Be an animal-doctor. Give the silly people up—if they haven't brains enough to see you're the best doctor in the world. Take care of animals instead—*they*'ll soon find it out. Be an animal-doctor."

"Oh, there are plenty of animal-doctors," said John Dolittle, putting the flower-pots outside on the window-sill to get the rain.

"Yes, there *are* plenty," said Polynesia. "But none of them are any good at all. Now listen, Doctor, and I'll tell you something. Did you know that animals can talk?"

"I knew that parrots can talk," said the Doctor.

"Oh, we parrots can talk in two languages—people's language and bird-language," said Polynesia proudly. "If I say, 'Polly wants a cracker,' you understand me. But hear this: *Ka-ka oi-ee, fee-fee?*"

"Good Gracious!" cried the Doctor. "What does that mean?"

"That means, 'Is the porridge hot yet?'—in bird-language."

"My! You don't say so!" said the Doctor. "You never talked that way to me before."

"What would have been the good?" said Polynesia, dusting some cracker-crumbs off her left wing. "You wouldn't have understood me if I had."

"Tell me some more," said the Doctor, all excited; and he rushed over to the dresser-drawer and came back with the butcher's book and a pencil. "Now don't go too fast—and I'll write it down. This is interesting—very interesting—something quite new. Give me the Birds' A.B.C. first—slowly now."

So that was the way the Doctor came to know that animals had a language of their own and could talk to one another. And all that afternoon, while it was raining, Polynesia sat on the kitchen table giving him bird words to put down in the book.

At tea-time, when the dog, Jip, came in, the parrot said to the Doctor, "See, *he's* talking to you."

"Looks to me as though he were scratching his ear," said the Doctor.

"But animals don't always speak with their mouths," said the parrot in a high voice, raising her eyebrows. "They talk with their ears, with their feet, with their tails—with everything. Sometimes they don't *want* to make a noise. Do you see now the way he's twitching up one side of his nose?"

"What's that mean?" asked the Doctor.

"That means, 'Can't you see that it has stopped raining?'" Polynesia answered. "He is asking you a question. Dogs nearly always use their noses for asking questions."

After a while, with the parrot's help, the Doctor got to learn the language of the animals so well that he could talk to them himself and understand everything they said. Then he gave up being a people's doctor altogether.

As soon as the Cat's-meat-Man had told every one that John Dolittle was going to become an animal-doctor, old ladies began to bring him their pet pugs and poodles who had eaten too much cake; and farmers came many miles to show him sick cows and sheep.

One day a plow-horse was brought to him; and the poor thing was terribly glad to find a man who could talk in horse-language.

"You know, Doctor," said the horse, "that vet

over the hill knows nothing at all. He has been treating me six weeks now—for spavins. What I need is *spectacles*. I am going blind in one eye. There's no reason why horses shouldn't wear glasses, the same as people. But that stupid man over the hill never even looked at my eyes. He kept on giving me big pills. I tried to tell him; but he couldn't understand a word of horse-language. What I need is spectacles."

"Of course—of course," said the Doctor. "I'll get you some at once."

"I would like a pair like yours," said the horse—"only green. They'll keep the sun out of my eyes while I'm plowing the Fifty-Acre Field."

"Certainly," said the Doctor. "Green ones you shall have."

"You know, the trouble is, Sir," said the plow-horse as the Doctor opened the front door to let him out—"the trouble is that *anybody* thinks he can doctor animals—just because the animals don't complain. As a matter of fact it takes a much cleverer man to be a really good animal-doctor than it does to be a good people's doctor. My farmer's boy thinks he knows all about horses. I wish you could see him—his face is so fat he looks as though he had no eyes—and he has got as much brain as a potato-bug. He tried to put a mustard-plaster on me last week."

"Where did he put it?" asked the Doctor.

"Oh, he didn't put it anywhere—on me," said the horse. "He only tried to. I kicked him into the duck-pond."

"Well, well!" said the Doctor.

"I'm a pretty quiet creature as a rule," said the horse—"very patient with people—don't make much fuss. But it was bad enough to have that vet giving me the wrong medicine. And when that red-faced booby started to monkey with me, I just couldn't bear it any more."

"Did you hurt the boy much?" asked the Doctor.

"Oh, no," said the horse. "I kicked him in the right place. The vet's looking after him now. When will my glasses be ready?"

"I'll have them for you next week," said the Doctor. "Come in again Tuesday—Good morning!"

Then John Dolittle got a fine, big pair of green spectacles; and the plow-horse stopped going blind in one eye and could see as well as ever.

And soon it became a common sight to see farm-animals wearing glasses in the country round Puddleby; and a blind horse was a thing unknown.

And so it was with all the other animals that were brought to him. As soon as they found that he could talk their language, they told him where the pain was and how they felt, and of course it was easy for him to cure them.

Now all these animals went back and told their brothers and friends that there was a doctor in the little house with the big garden who really *was* a doctor. And whenever any creatures got sick—not only horses and cows and dogs—but all the little things of the fields, like harvest-mice and water-voles, badgers and bats, they came at once to his house on the edge of the town, so that his big garden was nearly always crowded with animals trying to get in to see him.

There were so many that came that he had to have special doors made for the different kinds. He wrote "HORSES" over the front door, "COWS" over the side door, and "SHEEP" on the kitchen door. Each kind of animal had a separate door—even the mice had a tiny tunnel made for them into the cellar, where they waited patiently in rows for the Doctor to come round to them.

And so, in a few years' time, every living thing for miles and miles got to know about John Dolittle, M.D. And the birds who flew to other countries in the winter told the animals in foreign lands of the wonderful doctor of Puddleby-on-the-Marsh, who could understand their talk and help them in their troubles. In this way he became famous among the animals—all over the world—better known even than he had been among the folks of the West Country. And he was happy and liked his life very much.

One afternoon when the Doctor was busy writing in a book, Polynesia sat in the window—as she nearly always did—looking out at the leaves blowing about in the garden. Presently she laughed aloud.

"What is it, Polynesia?" asked the Doctor, looking up from his book.

"I was just thinking," said the parrot; and she went on looking at the leaves.

"What were you thinking?"

"I was thinking about people," said Polynesia. "People make me sick. They think they're so wonderful. The world has been going on now for thousands of years, hasn't it? And the only thing in animal-language that *people* have learned to understand is that when a dog wags his tail he means 'I'm glad!'—It's funny, isn't it? You are the very first man to talk like us. Oh, sometimes people annoy me dreadfully—such airs they put on—talking about 'the dumb animals.' *Dumb!*—Huh! Why I knew a macaw once who could say 'Good morning!' in seven different ways without once opening his mouth. He could talk every language—and Greek. An old professor with a gray beard bought him. But he didn't stay. He said the old man didn't talk Greek right, and he couldn't stand listening to him teach the language wrong. I often wonder what's become of him. That bird knew more geography than people will ever know.—*People,* Golly! I suppose if people ever learn to fly—like any common hedge-sparrow—we shall never hear the end of it!"

"You're a wise old bird," said the Doctor. "How old are you really? I know that parrots and elephants sometimes live to be very, very old."

"I can never be quite sure of my age," said Polynesia. "It's either a hundred and eighty-three or a hundred and eighty-two. But I know that when I first came here from Africa, King Charles was still hiding in the oak-tree—because I saw him. He looked scared to death."

THE THIRD CHAPTER

More Money Troubles

AND SOON NOW the Doctor began to make money again; and his sister, Sarah, bought a new dress and was happy.

Some of the animals who came to see him were so sick that they had to stay at the Doctor's house for a week. And when they were getting better they used to sit in chairs on the lawn.

And often even after they got well, they did not want to go away—they liked the Doctor and his house so much. And he never had the heart to refuse them when they asked if they could stay with him. So in this way he went on getting more and more pets.

Once when he was sitting on his garden wall, smoking a pipe in the evening, an Italian organ-grinder came round with a monkey on a string. The Doctor saw at once that the monkey's collar was too tight and that he was dirty and unhappy. So he took the monkey away from the Italian, gave the man a shilling and told him to go. The organ-grinder got awfully angry and said that he wanted to keep the monkey. But the Doctor told him that if he didn't go away he would punch him on the nose. John Dolittle was a strong man, though he wasn't very tall. So the Italian went away saying rude things and the monkey stayed with Doctor Dolittle and had a good home. The other animals in the house called him "Chee-Chee"—which is a common word in monkey-language, meaning "ginger."

And another time, when the circus came to Puddleby, the crocodile who had a bad toothache escaped at night and came into the Doctor's garden. The Doctor talked to him in crocodile-language and took him into the house and made his tooth better. But when the crocodile saw what a nice house it was —with all the different places for the different kinds of animals—he too wanted to live with the Doctor. He asked couldn't he sleep in the fish-pond at the bottom of the garden, if he promised not to eat the fish. When the circus-men came to take him back he got so wild and savage that he frightened them away. But to every one in the house he was always as gentle as a kitten.

But now the old ladies grew afraid to send their lap-dogs to Doctor Dolittle because of the crocodile; and the farmers wouldn't believe that he would not eat the lambs and sick calves they brought to be cured. So the Doctor went to the crocodile and told him he must go back to his circus. But he wept such big tears, and begged so hard to be allowed to stay, that the Doctor hadn't the heart to turn him out.

So then the Doctor's sister came to him and said,

"John, you must send that creature away. Now the farmers and the old ladies are afraid to send their animals to you—just as we were beginning to be well off again. Now we shall be ruined entirely. This is the last straw. I will no longer be housekeeper for you if you don't send away that alligator."

"It isn't an alligator," said the Doctor—"it's a crocodile."

"I don't care what you call it," said his sister. "It's a nasty thing to find under the bed. I won't have it in the house."

"But he has promised me," the Doctor answered, "that he will not bite any one. He doesn't like the circus; and I haven't the money to send him back to Africa where he comes from. He minds his own business and on the whole is very well behaved. Don't be so fussy."

"I tell you I *will not* have him around," said Sarah. "He eats the linoleum. If you don't send him away this minute I'll—I'll go and get married!"

"All right," said the Doctor, "go and get married.

It can't be helped." And he took down his hat and went out into the garden.

So Sarah Dolittle packed up her things and went off; and the Doctor was left all alone with his animal family.

And very soon he was poorer than he had ever been before. With all these mouths to fill, and the house to look after, and no one to do the mending, and no money coming in to pay the butcher's bill, things began to look very difficult. But the Doctor didn't worry at all.

"Money is a nuisance," he used to say. "We'd all be much better off if it had never been invented. What does money matter, so long as we are happy?"

But soon the animals themselves began to get worried. And one evening when the Doctor was asleep in his chair before the kitchen-fire they began talking it over among themselves in whispers. And the owl, Too-Too, who was good at arithmetic, figured it out that there was only money enough left to last another week—if they each had one meal a day and no more.

Then the parrot said, "I think we all ought to do the housework ourselves. At least we can do that much. After all, it is for our sakes that the old man finds himself so lonely and so poor."

So it was agreed that the monkey, Chee-Chee, was to do the cooking and mending; the dog was to sweep the floors; the duck was to dust and make the beds; the owl, Too-Too, was to keep the accounts, and the pig was to do the gardening. They made Polynesia, the parrot, housekeeper and laundress, because she was the oldest.

Of course at first they all found their new jobs very hard to do—all except Chee-Chee, who had hands, and could do things like a man. But they soon got used to it; and they used to think it great fun to watch Jip, the dog, sweeping his tail over the floor with a rag tied onto it for a broom. After a little they got to do the work so well that the Doctor said that he had never had his house kept so tidy or so clean before.

In this way things went along all right for a while; but without money they found it very hard.

Then the animals made a vegetable and flower stall outside the garden-gate and sold radishes and roses to the people that passed by along the road.

But still they didn't seem to make enough money to pay all the bills—and still the Doctor wouldn't worry. When the parrot came to him and told him that the fishmonger wouldn't give them any more fish, he said,

"Never mind. So long as the hens lay eggs and

the cow gives milk we can have omelettes and junket. And there are plenty of vegetables left in the garden. The Winter is still a long way off. Don't fuss. That was the trouble with Sarah—she would fuss. I wonder how Sarah's getting on—an excellent woman—in some ways—Well, well!"

But the snow came earlier than usual that year; and although the old lame horse hauled in plenty of wood from the forest outside the town, so they could have a big fire in the kitchen, most of the vegetables in the garden were gone, and the rest were covered with snow; and many of the animals were really hungry.

THE FOURTH CHAPTER

A Message from Africa

THAT WINTER was a very cold one. And one night in December, when they were all sitting round the warm fire in the kitchen, and the Doctor was reading aloud to them out of books he had written himself in animal-language, the owl, Too-Too, suddenly said,

"Sh! What's that noise outside?"

They all listened; and presently they heard the sound of some one running. Then the door flew open and the monkey, Chee-Chee, ran in, badly out of breath.

"Doctor!" he cried, "I've just had a message from a cousin of mine in Africa. There is a terrible sickness among the monkeys out there. They are all catching it—and they are dying in hundreds. They have heard of you, and beg you to come to Africa to stop the sickness."

"Who brought the message?" asked the Doctor, taking off his spectacles and laying down his book.

"A swallow," said Chee-Chee. "She is outside on the rain-butt."

"Bring her in by the fire," said the Doctor. "She must be perished with the cold. The swallows flew South six weeks ago!"

So the swallow was brought in, all huddled and shivering; and although she was a little afraid at first, she soon got warmed up and sat on the edge of the mantelpiece and began to talk.

When she had finished the Doctor said,

"I would gladly go to Africa—especially in this bitter weather. But I'm afraid we haven't money enough to buy the tickets. Get me the money-box, Chee-Chee."

So the monkey climbed up and got it off the top shelf of the dresser.

There was nothing in it—not one single penny!

"I felt sure there was twopence left," said the Doctor.

"There *was*," said the owl. "But you spent it on a rattle for that badger's baby when he was teething."

"Did I?" said the Doctor—"dear me, dear me! What a nuisance money is, to be sure! Well, never mind. Perhaps if I go down to the seaside I shall be able to borrow a boat that will take us to Africa. I knew a seaman once who brought his baby to me with measles. Maybe he'll lend us his boat—the baby got well."

So early the next morning the Doctor went down to the seashore. And when he came back he told the animals it was all right—the sailor was going to lend them the boat.

The the crocodile and the monkey and the parrot were very glad and began to sing, because they were going back to Africa, their real home. And the Doctor said,

"I shall only be able to take you three—with Jip the dog, Dab-Dab the duck, Gub-Gub the pig and the owl, Too-Too. The rest of the animals, like the dormice and the water-voles and the bats, they will have to go back and live in the fields where they were born till we come home again. But as most of them sleep through the Winter, they won't mind that —and besides, it wouldn't be good for them to go to Africa."

So then the parrot, who had been on long sea-voyages before, began telling the Doctor all the things he would have to take with him on the ship.

"You must have plenty of pilot-bread," she said —" 'hard tack' they call it. And you must have beef in cans—and an anchor."

"I expect the ship will have its own anchor," said the Doctor.

"Well, make sure," said Polynesia. "Because it's

very important. You can't stop if you haven't got an anchor. And you'll need a bell."

"What's that for?" asked the Doctor.

"To tell the time by," said the parrot. "You go and ring it every half-hour and then you know what time it is. And bring a whole lot of rope—it always comes in handy on voyages."

Then they began to wonder where they were going to get the money from to buy all the things they needed.

"Oh, bother it! Money again," cried the Doctor. "Goodness! I shall be glad to get to Africa where we don't have to have any! I'll go and ask the grocer if he will wait for his money till I get back—No, I'll send the sailor to ask him."

So the sailor went to see the grocer. And presently he came back with all the things they wanted.

Then the animals packed up; and after they had turned off the water so the pipes wouldn't freeze, and put up the shutters, they closed the house and gave the key to the old horse who lived in the stable. And when they had seen that there was plenty of hay in the loft to last the horse through the Winter, they carried all their luggage down to the seashore and got on to the boat.

The Cat's-meat-Man was there to see them off;

and he brought a large suet-pudding as a present for the Doctor because, he said he had been told, you couldn't get suet-puddings in foreign ports.

As soon as they were on the ship, Gub-Gub, the pig, asked where the beds were, for it was four o'clock in the afternoon and he wanted his nap. So Polynesia took him downstairs into the inside of the ship and showed him the beds, set all on top of one another like book-shelves against a wall.

"Why, that isn't a bed!" cried Gub-Gub. "That's a shelf!"

"Beds are always like that on ships," said the parrot. "It isn't a shelf. Climb up into it and go to sleep. That's what you call 'a bunk.'"

"I don't think I'll go to bed yet," said Gub-Gub. "I'm too excited. I want to go upstairs again and see them start."

"Well, this is your first trip," said Polynesia. "You will get used to the life after a while." And she went back up the stairs of the ship, humming this song to herself,

> I've seen the Black Sea and the Red Sea;
>   I rounded the Isle of Wight;
> I discovered the Yellow River,
>   And the Orange too—by night.

> Now Greenland drops behind again,
>   And I sail the ocean Blue.
> I'm tired of all these colors, Jane,
>   So I'm coming back to you.

They were just going to start on their journey, when the Doctor said he would have to go back and ask the sailor the way to Africa.

But the swallow said she had been to that country many times and would show them how to get there.

So the Doctor told Chee-Chee to pull up the anchor and the voyage began.

THE FIFTH CHAPTER

The Great Journey

NOW FOR SIX WHOLE WEEKS they went sailing on and on, over the rolling sea, following the swallow who flew before the ship to show them the way. At night she carried a tiny lantern, so they should not miss her in the dark; and the people on the other ships that passed said that the light must be a shooting star.

As they sailed further and further into the South, it got warmer and warmer. Polynesia, Chee-Chee and the crocodile enjoyed the hot sun no end. They ran about laughing and looking over the side of the ship to see if they could see Africa yet.

But the pig and the dog and the owl, Too-Too, could do nothing in such weather, but sat at the end of the ship in the shade of a big barrel, with their tongues hanging out, drinking lemonade.

Dab-Dab, the duck, used to keep herself cool by jumping into the sea and swimming behind the ship. And every once in a while, when the top of her head got too hot, she would dive under the ship and come up on the other side. In this way, too, she used to catch herrings on Tuesdays and Fridays—when everybody on the boat ate fish to make the beef last longer.

When they got near to the Equator they saw some flying-fishes coming towards them. And the fishes asked the parrot if this was Doctor Dolittle's ship. When she told them it was, they said they were glad, because the monkeys in Africa were getting worried that he would never come. Polynesia asked them how many miles they had yet to go; and the flying-fishes said it was only fifty-five miles now to the coast of Africa.

And another time a whole school of porpoises came dancing through the waves; and they too asked Polynesia if this was the ship of the famous doctor. And when they heard that it was, they asked the parrot if the Doctor wanted anything for his journey.

And Polynesia said, "Yes. We have run short of onions."

"There is an island not far from here," said the porpoises, "where the wild onions grow tall and strong. Keep straight on—we will get some and catch up to you."

So the porpoises dashed away through the sea. And very soon the parrot saw them again, coming up behind, dragging the onions through the waves in big nets made of seaweed.

The next evening, as the sun was going down, the Doctor said,

"Get me the telescope, Chee-Chee. Our journey is nearly ended. Very soon we should be able to see the shores of Africa."

And about half an hour later, sure enough, they thought they could see something in front that might be land. But it began to get darker and darker and they couldn't be sure.

Then a great storm came up, with thunder and lightning. The wind howled; the rain came down in torrents; and the waves got so high they splashed right over the boat.

Presently there was a big BANG! The ship stopped and rolled over on its side.

"What's happened?" asked the Doctor, coming up from downstairs.

"I'm not sure," said the parrot; "but I think we're ship-wrecked. Tell the duck to get out and see."

So Dab-Dab dived right down under the waves. And when she came up she said they had struck a rock; there was a big hole in the bottom of the ship; the water was coming in; and they were sinking fast.

"We must have run into Africa," said the Doctor.

"Dear me, dear me!—Well—we must all swim to land."

But Chee-Chee and Gub-Gub did not know how to swim.

"Get the rope!" said Polynesia. "I told you it would come in handy. Where's that duck? Come here, Dab-Dab. Take this end of the rope, fly to the shore and tie it on to a palm-tree; and we'll hold the other end on the ship here. Then those that can't swim must climb along the rope till they reach the land. That's what you call a 'life-line.' "

So they all got safely to the shore—some swimming, some flying; and those that climbed along the rope brought the Doctor's trunk and handbag with them.

But the ship was no good any more—with the big hole in the bottom; and presently the rough sea beat it to pieces on the rocks and the timbers floated away.

Then they all took shelter in a nice dry cave they found, high up in the cliffs, till the storm was over.

When the sun came out next morning they went down to the sandy beach to dry themselves.

"Dear old Africa!" sighed Polynesia. "It's good to get back. Just think—it'll be a hundred and sixty-nine years to-morrow since I was here! And it hasn't changed a bit! Same old palm-trees; same old red earth; same old black ants! There's no place like home!"

And the others noticed she had tears in her eyes—she was so pleased to see her country once again.

Then the Doctor missed his high hat; for it had been blown into the sea during the storm. So Dab-Dab went out to look for it. And presently she saw it, a long way off, floating on the water like a toy-boat.

When she flew down to get it, she found one of the white mice, very frightened, sitting inside it.

"What are you doing here?" asked the duck. "You were told to stay behind in Puddleby."

"I didn't want to be left behind," said the mouse. "I wanted to see what Africa was like—I have relatives there. So I hid in the baggage and was brought on to the ship with the hard-tack. When the ship sank I was terribly frightened—because I cannot swim far. I swam as long as I could, but I soon got all exhausted and thought I was going to sink. And then, just at that moment, the old man's hat came floating by; and I got into it because I did not want to be drowned."

So the duck took up the hat with the mouse in it and brought it to the Doctor on the shore. And they all gathered round to have a look.

"That's what you call a 'stowaway,'" said the parrot.

Presently, when they were looking for a place in the trunk where the white mouse could travel comfortably, the monkey, Chee-Chee, suddenly said,

"Sh! I hear footsteps in the jungle!"

They all stopped talking and listened. And soon a black man came down out of the woods and asked them what they were doing there.

"My name is John Dolittle—M.D.," said the Doctor. "I have been asked to come to Africa to cure the monkeys who are sick."

"You must all come before the King," said the black man.

"What king?" asked the Doctor, who didn't want to waste any time.

"The King of the Jolliginki," the man answered. "All these lands belong to him; and all strangers must be brought before him. Follow me."

So they gathered up their baggage and went off, following the man through the jungle.

THE SIXTH CHAPTER

Polynesia and the King

WHEN THEY HAD GONE A LITTLE WAY through the thick forest they came to a wide, clear space; and they saw the King's palace which was made of mud.

This was where the King lived with his Queen, Ermintrude, and their son, Prince Bumpo. The Prince was away fishing for salmon in the river. But the King and Queen were sitting under an umbrella before the palace door. And Queen Ermintrude was asleep.

When the Doctor had come up to the palace the King asked him his business; and the Doctor told him why he had come to Africa.

"You may not travel through my lands," said the King. "Many years ago a white man came to these shores; and I was very kind to him. But after he had dug holes in the ground to get the gold, and killed all the elephants to get their ivory tusks, he went away secretly in his ship—without so much as saying 'Thank you.' Never again shall a white man travel through the lands of Jolliginki."

Then the King turned to some of the black men who were standing near and said, "Take away this medicine-man—with all his animals, and lock them up in my strongest prison."

So six of the black men led the Doctor and all his pets away and shut them up in a stone dungeon. The dungeon had only one little window, high up in the wall, with bars in it; and the door was strong and thick.

Then they all grew very sad; and Gub-Gub, the pig, began to cry. But Chee-Chee said he would spank him if he didn't stop that horrible noise; and he kept quiet.

"Are we all here?" asked the Doctor, after he had got used to the dim light.

"Yes, I think so," said the duck and started to count them.

"Where's Poylnesia?" asked the crocodile. "She isn't here."

"Are you sure?" said the Doctor. "Look again. Polynesia! Polynesia! Where are you?"

"I suppose she escaped," grumbled the crocodile. "Well, that's just like her!—Sneaked off into the jungle as soon as her friends got into trouble."

"I'm not that kind of a bird," said the parrot, climbing out of the pocket in the tail of the Doctor's coat. "You see, I'm small enough to get through the bars of that window; and I was afraid they would put me in a cage instead. So while the King was busy talking, I hid in the Doctor's pocket—and here I am! That's what you call a 'ruse,'" she said, smoothing down her feathers with her beak.

"Good Gracious!" cried the Doctor. "You're lucky I didn't sit on you."

"Now listen," said Polynesia, "to-night, as soon as it gets dark, I am going to creep through the bars of that window and fly over to the palace. And then —you'll see—I'll soon find a way to make the King let us all out of prison."

"Oh, what can *you* do?" said Gub-Gub, turning up his nose and beginning to cry again. "You're only a bird!"

"Quite true," said the parrot. "But do not forget that although I am only a bird, *I can talk like a man* —and I know these people."

So that night, when the moon was shining through the palm-trees and all the King's men were asleep, the parrot slipped out through the bars of the prison and flew across to the palace. The pantry window had been broken by a tennis ball the week before; and Polynesia popped in through the hole in the glass.

She heard Prince Bumpo snoring in his bedroom at the back of the palace. Then she tip-toed up the stairs till she came to the King's bedroom. She opened the door gently and peeped in.

The Queen was away at a dance that night at her cousin's; but the King was in bed fast asleep.

Polynesia crept in, very softly, and got under the bed.

Then she coughed—just the way Doctor Dolittle used to cough. Polynesia could mimic any one.

The King opened his eyes and said sleepily: "Is that you, Ermintrude?" (He thought it was the Queen come back from the dance.)

Then the parrot coughed again—loud, like a man. And the King sat up, wide awake, and said, "Who's that?"

"I am Doctor Dolittle," said the parrot—just the way the Doctor would have said it.

"What are you doing in my bedroom?" cried the King. "How dare you get out of prison! Where are you?—I don't see you."

But the parrot just laughed—a long, deep jolly laugh, like the Doctor's.

"Stop laughing and come here at once, so I can see you," said the King.

"Foolish King!" answered Polynesia. "Have you forgotten that you are talking to John Dolittle, M.D. —the most wonderful man on earth? Of course you cannot see me. I have made myself invisible. There is nothing I cannot do. Now listen: I have come here to-night to warn you. If you don't let me and my animals travel through your kingdom, I will make you and all your people sick like the monkeys. For I can make people well: and I can make people ill—just by raising my little finger. Send your soldiers at once to open the dungeon door, or you shall have mumps before the morning sun has risen on the hills of Jolliginki."

Then the King began to tremble and was very much afraid.

"Doctor," he cried, "it shall be as you say. Do not raise your little finger, please!" And he jumped out of bed and ran to tell the soldiers to open the prison door.

As soon as he was gone, Polynesia crept downstairs and left the palace by the pantry window.

But the Queen, who was just letting herself in at the backdoor with a latch-key, saw the parrot getting out through the broken glass. And when the King came back to bed she told him what she had seen.

Then the King understood that he had been tricked, and he was dreadfully angry. He hurried back to the prison at once.

But he was too late. The door stood open. The dungeon was empty. The Doctor and all his animals were gone.

THE SEVENTH CHAPTER

The Bridge of Apes

QUEEN ERMINTRUDE had never in her life seen her husband so terrible as he got that night. He gnashed his teeth with rage. He called everybody a fool. He threw his tooth-brush at the palace cat. He rushed round in his night-shirt and woke up all his army and sent them into the jungle to catch the Doctor. Then he made all his servants go too—his cooks and his gardeners and his barber and Prince Bumpo's tutor—even the Queen, who was tired from dancing in a pair of tight shoes, was packed off to help the soldiers in their search.

All this time the Doctor and his animals were running through the forest towards the Land of the Monkeys as fast as they could go.

Gub-Gub, with his short legs, soon got tired; and the Doctor had to carry him—which made it pretty hard when they had the trunk and the hand-bag with them as well.

The King of the Jolliginki thought it would be easy for his army to find them, because the Doctor was in a strange land and would not know his way.

But he was wrong; because the monkey, Chee-Chee, knew all the paths through the jungle—better even than the King's men did. And he led the Doctor and his pets to the very thickest part of the forest—a place where no man had ever been before—and hid them all in a big hollow tree between high rocks.

"We had better wait here," said Chee-Chee, "till the soldiers have gone back to bed. Then we can go on into the Land of the Monkeys."

So there they stayed the whole night through.

They often heard the King's men searching and talking in the jungle round about. But they were quite safe, for no one knew of that hiding-place but Chee-Chee—not even the other monkeys.

At last, when daylight began to come through the thick leaves overhead, they heard Queen Ermintrude saying in a very tired voice that it was no use looking any more—that they might as well go back and get some sleep.

As soon as the soldiers had all gone home, Chee-Chee brought the Doctor and his animals out of the hiding-place and they set off for the Land of the Monkeys.

It was a long, long way; and they often got very tired—especially Gub-Gub. But when he cried they gave him milk out of the cocoanuts which he was very fond of.

They always had plenty to eat and drink; because Chee-Chee and Polynesia knew all the different kinds of fruits and vegetables that grow in the jungle, and where to find them—like dates and figs and ground-nuts and ginger and yams. They used to make their lemonade out of the juice of wild oranges, sweetened with honey which they got from the bees' nests in hollow trees. No matter what it was they asked for, Chee-Chee and Polynesia always seemed to be able to get it for them—or something like it. They even got the Doctor some tobacco one day, when he had finished what he had brought with him and wanted to smoke.

At night they slept in tents made of palm-leaves, on thick, soft beds of dried grass. And after a while they got used to walking such a lot and did not get so tired and enjoyed the life of travel very much.

But they were always glad when the night came and they stopped for their resting-time. Then the Doctor used to make a little fire of sticks; and after they had had their supper, they would sit round it in a ring, listening to Polynesia singing songs about the sea, or to Chee-Chee telling stories of the jungle.

And many of the tales that Chee-Chee told were very interesting. Because although the monkeys had no history-books of their own before Doctor Dolittle came to write them for them, they remember everything that happens by telling stories to their children. And Chee-Chee spoke of many things his grandmother had told him—tales of long, long, long ago, before Noah and the Flood—of the days when men dressed in bear-skins and lived in holes in the rock and ate their mutton raw, because they did not know what cooking was—having never seen a fire. And he told them of the Great Mammoths and Lizards, as long as a train, that wandered over the mountains in those times, nibbling from the tree-tops. And often they got so interested listening, that when he had finished they found their fire had gone right out; and they had to scurry round to get more sticks and build a new one.

Now when the King's army had gone back and told the King that they couldn't find the Doctor, the King sent them out again and told them they must stay in the jungle till they caught him. So all this time, while the Doctor and his animals were going along towards the Land of the Monkeys, thinking themselves quite safe, they were still being followed by the King's men. If Chee-Chee had known this, he would most likely have hidden them again. But he didn't know it.

One day Chee-Chee climbed up a high rock and looked out over the tree-tops. And when he came down he said they were now quite close to the Land of the Monkeys and would soon be there.

And that same evening, sure enough, they saw Chee-Chee's cousin and a lot of other monkeys, who had not yet got sick, sitting in the trees by the edge of a swamp, looking and waiting for them. And when they saw the famous doctor really come, these monkeys made a tremendous noise, cheering and waving leaves and swinging out of the branches to greet him.

They wanted to carry his bag and his trunk and everything he had—and one of the bigger ones even carried Gub-Gub who had got tired again. Then two of them rushed on in front to tell the sick monkeys that the great doctor had come at last.

But the King's men, who were still following, had heard the noise of the monkeys cheering; and they at last knew where the Doctor was, and hastened on to catch him.

The big monkey carrying Gub-Gub was coming along behind slowly, and he saw the Captain of the army sneaking through the trees. So he hurried after the Doctor and told him to run.

Then they all ran harder than they had ever run in their lives; and the King's men, coming after them, began to run too; and the Captain ran hardest of all.

Then the Doctor tripped over his medicine-bag and fell down in the mud, and the Captain thought he would surely catch him this time.

But the Captain had very long ears—though his hair was very short. And as he sprang forward to take hold of the Doctor, one of his ears caught fast in a tree; and the rest of the army had to stop and help him.

By this time the Doctor had picked himself up, and on they went again, running and running. And Chee-Chee shouted,

"It's all right! We haven't far to go now!"

But before they could get into the Land of the Monkeys, they came to a steep cliff with a river flowing below. This was the end of the kingdom of Jolliginki; and the Land of the Monkeys was on the other side—across the river.

And Jip, the dog, looked down over the edge of the steep, steep cliff and said,

"Golly! How are we ever going to get across?"

"Oh, dear!" said Gub-Gub. "The King's men are quite close now—Look at them! I am afraid we are going to be taken back to prison again." And he began to weep.

But the big monkey who was carrying the pig dropped him on the ground and cried out to the other monkeys.

"Boys—a bridge! Quick!—Make a bridge! We've only a minute to do it. They've got the Captain loose, and he's coming on like a deer. Get lively! A bridge! A bridge!"

The Doctor began to wonder what they were going to make a bridge out of, and he gazed around to see if they had any boards hidden any place.

But when he looked back at the cliff, there, hanging across the river, was a bridge all ready for him—made of living monkeys! For while his back was turned, the monkeys—quick as a flash—had made themselves into a bridge, just by holding hands and feet.

And the big one shouted to the Doctor, "Walk over! Walk over—all of you—hurry!"

Gub-Gub was a bit scared, walking on such a narrow bridge at that dizzy height above the river. But he got over all right; and so did all of them.

John Dolittle was the last to cross. And just as he was getting to the other side, the King's men came rushing up to the edge of the cliff.

Then they shook their fists and yelled with rage. For they saw they were too late. The Doctor and all his animals were safe in the Land of the Monkeys and the bridge was pulled across to the other side.

Then Chee-Chee turned to the Doctor and said, "Many great explorers and gray-bearded naturalists have lain long weeks hidden in the jungle waiting to see the monkeys do that trick. But we never let a white man get a glimpse of it before. You are the first to see the famous 'Bridge of Apes.' "

And the Doctor felt very pleased.

THE EIGHTH CHAPTER

The Leader of the Lions

JOHN DOLITTLE now became dreadfully, awfully busy. He found hundreds and thousands of monkeys sick—gorillas, orangoutangs, chimpanzees, dog-faced baboons, marmosettes, gray monkeys, red ones—all kinds. And many had died.

The first thing he did was to separate the sick ones from the well ones. Then he got Chee-Chee and his cousin to build him a little house of grass. The next thing: he made all the monkeys who were still well come and be vaccinated.

And for three days and three nights the monkeys kept coming from the jungles and the valleys and the hills to the little house of grass, where the Doctor sat all day and all night, vaccinating and vaccinating.

Then he had another house made—a big one, with a lot of beds in it; and he put all the sick ones in this house.

But so many were sick, there were not enough well ones to do the nursing. So he sent messages to the other animals, like the lions and the leopards and the antelopes, to come and help with the nursing.

But the Leader of the Lions was a very proud creature. And when he came to the Doctor's big house full of beds he seemed angry and scornful.

"Do you dare to ask me, Sir?" he said, glaring at the Doctor. "Do you dare to ask me—*ME, the King of Beasts,* to wait on a lot of dirty monkeys? Why, I wouldn't even eat them between meals!"

Although the lion looked very terrible, the Doctor tried hard not to seem afraid of him.

"I didn't ask you to eat them," he said quietly. "And besides, they're not dirty. They've all had a bath this morning. *Your* coat looks as though it needed brushing—badly. Now listen, and I'll tell you something: the day may come when the lions get sick. And if you don't help the other animals now, the lions may find themselves left all alone when *they* are in trouble. That often happens to proud people."

"The lions are never *in* trouble—they only *make* trouble," said the Leader, turning up his nose. And he stalked away into the jungle, feeling he had been rather smart and clever.

Then the leopards got proud too and said they wouldn't help. And then of course the antelopes—although they were too shy and timid to be rude to the Doctor like the lion—*they* pawed the ground, and smiled foolishly, and said they had never been nurses before.

And now the poor Doctor was worried frantic, wondering where he could get help enough to take care of all these thousands of monkeys in bed.

But the Leader of the Lions, when he got back to his den, saw his wife, the Queen Lioness, come running out to meet him with her hair untidy.

"One of the cubs won't eat," she said. "I don't know *what* to do with him. He hasn't taken a thing since last night."

And she began to cry and shake with nervousness —for she was a good mother, even though she was a lioness.

So the Leader went into his den and looked at his children—two very cunning little cubs, lying on the floor. And one of them seemed quite poorly.

Then the lion told his wife, quite proudly, just what he had said to the Doctor. And she got so angry she nearly drove him out of the den.

"You never *did* have a grain of sense!" she screamed. "All the animals from here to the Indian Ocean are talking about this wonderful man, and how he can cure any kind of sickness, and how kind he is—the only man in the whole world who can talk the language of the animals! And now, *now*— when we have a sick baby on our hands, you must go and offend him! You great booby! Nobody but a fool is ever rude to a *good* doctor. You—," and she started pulling her husband's hair.

"Go back to that white man at once," she yelled, "and tell him you're sorry. And take all the other empty-headed lions with you—and those stupid leopards and antelopes. Then do everything the Doctor tells you. Work hard! And perhaps he will be kind enough to come and see the cub later. Now be off!—*Hurry,* I tell you! You're not fit to be a father!"

And she went into the den next door, where another mother-lion lived, and told her all about it.

So the Leader of the Lions went back to the Doctor and said, "I happened to be passing this way and thought I'd look in. Got any help yet?"

"No," said the Doctor. "I haven't. And I'm dreadfully worried."

"Help's pretty hard to get these days," said the lion. "Animals don't seem to want to work any more. You can't blame them—in a way. . . . Well, seeing you're in difficulties, I don't mind doing what I can —just to oblige you—so long as I don't have to wash the creatures. And I have told all the other hunting animals to come and do their share. The leopards should be here any minute now. . . . Oh, and by the way, we've got a sick cub at home. I don't think there's much the matter with him myself. But the wife is anxious. If you are around that way this evening, you might take a look at him, will you?"

Then the Doctor was very happy; for all the lions and the leopards and the antelopes and the giraffes and the zebras—all the animals of the forests and the mountains and the plains—came to help him in his work. There were so many of them that he had to send some away, and only kept the cleverest.

And now very soon the monkeys began to get better. At the end of a week the big house full of beds was half empty. And at the end of the second week the last monkey had got well.

Then the Doctor's work was done; and he was so tired he went to bed and slept for three days without even turning over.

THE NINTH CHAPTER

The Monkey's Council

CHEE-CHEE stood outside the Doctor's door, keeping everybody away till he woke up. Then John Dolittle told the monkeys that he must now go back to Puddleby.

They were very surprised at this; for they had thought that he was going to stay with them forever. And that night all the monkeys got together in the jungle to talk it over.

And the Chief Chimpanzee rose up and said,

"Why is it the good man is going away? Is he not happy here with us?"

But none of them could answer him.

Then the Grand Gorilla got up and said,

"I think we all should go to him and ask him to stay. Perhaps if we make him a new house and a bigger bed, and promise him plenty of monkey-servants to work for him and to make life pleasant for him—perhaps then he will not wish to go."

Then Chee-Chee got up; and all the others whispered, "Sh! Look! Chee-Chee, the great Traveler, is about to speak!"

And Chee-Chee said to the other monkeys,

"My friends, I am afraid it is useless to ask the Doctor to stay. He owes money in Puddleby; and he says he must go back and pay it."

And the monkeys asked him, "What is *money?*"

Then Chee-Chee told them that in the Land of the White Men you could get nothing without money; you could *do* nothing without money—that it was almost impossible to *live* without money.

And some of them asked, "But can you not even eat and drink without paying?"

But Chee-Chee shook his head. And then he told them that even he, when he was with the organ-grinder, had been made to ask the children for money.

And the Chief Chimpanzee turned to the Oldest Orangoutang and said, "Cousin, surely these Men be strange creatures! Who would wish to live in such a land? My gracious, how paltry!"

Then Chee-Chee said,

"When we were coming to you we had no boat to cross the sea in and no money to buy food to eat on our journey. So a man lent us some biscuits; and we said we would pay him when we came back. And we borrowed a boat from a sailor; but it was broken on the rocks when we reached the shores of Africa. Now the Doctor says he must go back and get the sailor another boat—because the man was poor and his ship was all he had."

And the monkeys were all silent for a while, sitting quite still upon the ground and thinking hard.

At last the Biggest Baboon got up and said,

"I do not think we ought to let this good man leave our land till we have given him a fine present to take with him, so that he may know we are grateful for all that he has done for us."

And a little, tiny red monkey who was sitting up in a tree shouted down,

"I think that too!"

And then they all cried out, making a great noise, "Yes, yes. Let us give him the finest present a White Man ever had!"

Now they began to wonder and ask one another what would be the best thing to give him. And one said, "Fifty bags of cocoanuts!" And another—"A hundred bunches of bananas!—At least he shall not have to buy his fruit in the Land Where You Pay to Eat!"

But Chee-Chee told them that all these things would be too heavy to carry so far and would go bad before half was eaten.

"If you want to please him," he said, "give him an animal. You may be sure he will be kind to it. Give him some rare animal they have not got in the menageries."

And the monkeys asked him, "What are *menageries?*"

Then Chee-Chee explained to them that menageries were places in the Land of the White Men, where animals were put in cages for people to come and look at. And the monkeys were very shocked and said to one another,

"These Men are like thoughtless young ones—stupid and easily amused. Sh! It is a prison he means."

So then they asked Chee-Chee what rare animal it could be that they should give the Doctor—one the White Men had not seen before. And the Major of the Marmosettes asked,

"Have they an iguana over there?"

But Chee-Chee said, "Yes, there is one in the London Zoo."

And another asked, "Have they an okapi?"

But Chee-Chee said, "Yes. In Belgium, where my organ-grinder took me five years ago, they had an okapi in a big city they call Antwerp."

And another asked, "Have they a pushmi-pullyu?"

Then Chee-Chee said, "No. No White Man has ever seen a pushmi-pullyu. Let us give him that."

THE TENTH CHAPTER

The Rarest Animal of All

PUSHMI-PULLYUS are now extinct. That means, there aren't any more. But long ago, when Doctor Dolittle was alive, there were some of them still left in the deepest jungles of Africa; and even then they were very, very scarce. They had no tail, but a head at each end, and sharp horns on each head. They were very shy and terribly hard to catch. The black men get most of their animals by sneaking up behind them while they are not looking. But you could not do this with the pushmi-pullyu—because, no matter which way you came towards him, he was always facing you. And besides, only one half of him slept at a time. The other head was always awake—and watching. This was why they were never caught and never seen in Zoos. Though many of the greatest huntsmen and the cleverest menagerie-keepers spent years of their lives searching through the jungles in all weathers for pushmi-pullyus, not a single one had ever been caught. Even then, years ago, he was the only animal in the world with two heads.

Well, the monkeys set out hunting for this animal through the forest. And after they had gone a good many miles, one of them found peculiar footprints near the edge of a river; and they knew that a pushmi-pullyu must be very near that spot.

Then they went along the bank of the river a little way and they saw a place where the grass was high and thick; and they guessed that he was in there.

So they all joined hands and made a great circle round the high grass. The pushmi-pullyu heard them coming; and he tried hard to break through the ring of monkeys. But he couldn't do it. When he saw that it was no use trying to escape, he sat down and waited to see what they wanted.

They asked him if he would go with Doctor Dolittle and be put on show in the Land of the White Men.

But he shook both his heads hard and said, "Certainly not!"

They explained to him that he would not be shut up in a menagerie but would just be looked at. They told him that the Doctor was a very kind man but hadn't any money; and people would pay to see a two-headed animal and the Doctor would get rich and could pay for the boat he had borrowed to come to Africa in.

But he answered, "No. You know how shy I am—I hate being stared at." And he almost began to cry.

Then for three days they tried to persuade him. And at the end of the third day he said he would come with them and see what kind of a man the Doctor was, first.

So the monkeys traveled back with the pushmi-pullyu. And when they came to where the Doctor's little house of grass was, they knocked on the door.

The duck, who was packing the trunk, said, "Come in!"

And Chee-Chee very proudly took the animal inside and showed him to the Doctor.

"What in the world is it?" asked John Dolittle, gazing at the strange creature.

"Lord save us!" cried the duck. "How does it make up its mind?"

"It doesn't look to me as though it had any," said Jip, the dog.

"This, Doctor," said Chee-Chee, "is the pushmi-pullyu—the rarest animal of the African jungles, the only two-headed beast in the world! Take him home with you and your fortune's made. People will pay any money to see him."

"But I don't want any money," said the Doctor.

"Yes, you do," said Dab-Dab, the duck. "Don't

you remember how we had to pinch and scrape to to pay the butcher's bill in Puddleby? And how are you going to get the sailor the new boat you spoke of—unless we have the money to buy it?"

"I was going to make him one," said the Doctor.

"Oh, do be sensible!" cried Dab-Dab. "Where would you get all the wood and the nails to make one with?—And besides, what are we going to live on? We shall be poorer than ever when we get back. Chee-Chee's perfectly right: take the funny-looking thing along, do!"

"Well, perhaps there is something in what you say," murmured the Doctor. "It certainly would make a nice new kind of pet. But does the er—what-do-you-call-it really want to go abroad?"

"Yes, I'll go," said the pushmi-pullyu who saw at once, from the Doctor's face, that he was a man to be trusted. "You have been so kind to the animals here—and the monkeys tell me that I am the only one who will do. But you must promise me that if I do not like it in the Land of the White Men you will send me back."

"Why, certainly—of course, of course," said the Doctor. "Excuse me, surely you are related to the Deer Family, are you not?"

"Yes," said the pushmi-pullyu—"to the Abyssinian Gazelles and the Asiatic Chamois—on my mother's side. My father's great-grandfather was the last of the Unicorns."

"Most interesting!" murmured the Doctor; and he took a book out of the trunk which Dab-Dab was packing and began turning the pages. "Let us see if Buffon says anything—"

"I notice," said the duck, "that you only talk with one of your mouths. Can't the other head talk as well?"

"Oh, yes," said the pushmi-pullyu. "But I keep the other mouth for eating—mostly. In that way I can talk while I am eating without being rude. Our people have always been very polite."

When the packing was finished and everything was ready to start, the monkeys gave a grand party for the Doctor, and all the animals of the jungle came. And they had pineapples and mangoes and honey and all sorts of good things to eat and drink.

After they had all finished eating, the Doctor got up and said,

"My friends: I am not clever at speaking long words after dinner, like some men; and I have just eaten many fruits and much honey. But I wish to tell you that I am very sad at leaving your beautiful country. Because I have things to do in the Land of the White Men, I must go. After I have gone, remember never to let the flies settle on your food before you eat it; and do not sleep on the ground when the rains are coming. I—er—er—I hope you will all live happily ever after."

When the Doctor stopped speaking and sat down, all the monkeys clapped their hands a long time and said to one another, "Let it be remembered always among our people that he sat and ate with us, here, under the trees. For surely he is the Greatest of Men!"

And the Grand Gorilla, who had the strength of seven horses in his hairy arms, rolled a great rock up to the head of the table and said,

"This stone for all time shall mark the spot."

And even to this day, in the heart of the jungle, that stone still is there. And monkey-mothers, passing through the forest with their families, still point down at it from the branches and whisper to their children, "Sh! There it is—look—where the Good White Man sat and ate food with us in the Year of the Great Sickness!"

Then, when the party was over, the Doctor and his pets started out to go back to the seashore. And all the monkeys went with him as far as the edge of their country, carrying his trunk and bags, to see him off.

THE LAST CHAPTER

Home Again

MARCH WINDS had come and gone; April's showers were over; May's buds had opened into flower; and the June sun was shining on the pleasant fields, when John Dolittle at last got back to his own country.

But he did not yet go home to Puddleby. First he went traveling through the land with the pushmi-pullyu in a gipsy-wagon, stopping at all the country-fairs. And there, with the acrobats on one side of them and the Punch-and-Judy show on the other, they would hang out a big sign which read, "COME AND SEE THE MARVELOUS TWO-HEADED ANIMAL FROM THE JUNGLES OF AFRICA. Admisssion SIX-PENCE."

And the pushmi-pullyu would stay inside the wagon, while the other animals would lie about underneath. The Doctor sat in a chair in front taking the sixpences and smiling on the people as they went in; and Dab-Dab was kept busy all the time scolding him because he would let the children in for nothing when she wasn't looking.

And menagerie-keepers and circus-men came and asked the Doctor to sell them the strange creature, saying they would pay a tremendous lot of money for him. But the Doctor always shook his head and said,

"No. The pushmi-pullyu shall never be shut up in a cage. He shall be free always to come and go, like you and me."

Many curious sights and happenings they saw in this wandering life; but they all seemed quite ordinary after the great things they had seen and done in foreign lands. It was very interesting at first, being sort of part of a circus; but after a few weeks they all got dreadfully tired of it and the Doctor and all of them were longing to go home.

But so many people came flocking to the little wagon and paid the sixpence to go inside and see the pushmi-pullyu that very soon the Doctor was able to give up being a showman.

And one fine day, when the hollyhocks were in full bloom, he came back to Puddleby a rich man, to live in the little house with the big garden.

And the old lame horse in the stable was glad to see him; and so were the swallows who had already built their nests under the eaves of his roof and had young ones. And Dab-Dab was glad, too, to get back to the house she knew so well—although there was a terrible lot of dusting to be done, with cobwebs everywhere.

And after Jip had gone and shown his golden collar to the conceited collie next-door, he came back and began running round the garden like a crazy thing, looking for the bones he had buried long ago, and chasing the rats out of the tool-shed; while Gub-Gub dug up the horse-radish which had grown three feet high in the corner by the garden-wall.

And the Doctor went and saw the sailor who had lent him the boat, and he bought two new ships for him and a rubber-doll for his baby; and he paid the grocer for the food he had lent him for the journey to Africa. And he bought another piano and put the white mice back in it—because they said the bureau-drawer was drafty.

Even when the Doctor had filled the old money-box on the dresser-shelf, he still had a lot of money left; and he had to get three more money-boxes, just as big, to put the rest in.

"Money," he said, "is a terrible nuisance. But it's nice not to have to worry."

"Yes," said Dab-Dab, who was toasting muffins for his tea, "it is indeed!"

And when the Winter came again, and the snow flew against the kitchen-window, the Doctor and his animals would sit round the big, warm fire after supper; and he would read aloud to them out of his books.

But far away in Africa, where the monkeys chattered in the palm-trees before they went to bed under the big yellow moon, they would say to one another,

"I wonder what The Good Man's doing now—over there, in the Land of the White Men! Do you think he ever will come back?"

And Polynesia would squeak out from the vines,

"I think he will—I guess he will—I hope he will!"

And then the crocodile would grunt up at them from the black mud of the river,

"I'm SURE he will—Go to sleep!"

THE GOLDFISH

There was once a Goldfish who lived in the sea in the days when all fishes lived there. He was perfectly happy, and had only one care; and that was to avoid the net that floated about in the water, now here, now there. But all the fish had been warned by King Neptune, their father, to avoid the net, and in those days they did as they were bid. So the Goldfish enjoyed a glorious life, swimming for days and days in the blue and green water: sometimes low down close to the sand and shells and pearls and coral, and the big rocks where the anemones grew like clusters of gay flowers, and the seaweed waved in frills and fans of red and green and yellow; and sometimes he swam high up near the surface of the sea, where the white caps chased each other and the great waves rose like mountains of glass and tumbled over themselves with a crash. When the Goldfish was as near the top as this, he sometimes saw swimming in the bright blue water far, far above him a great Gold Fish, as golden as himself but as round as a jelly-fish. And at other times, when that distant water was dark blue instead of bright, he saw a Silver Fish such as he had never met under the sea, and she too was often round in shape, though at times, when she seemed to swim sideways through the water, he could see her pointed silver fins. Our Goldfish felt a certain jealousy of the other Gold Fish, but with the Silver Fish he fell in love at sight and longed to be able to swim up to her. Whenever he tried to do this, something queer happened that made him lose his breath; and with a gasp he sank down into the ocean, so deep that he could see the Silver Fish no longer. Then, hoping she might descend to swim in his own water, he swam for miles and miles in search of her; but he never had the luck to find her.

One night as he was swimming about in very calm water, he saw overhead the motionless shadow of an enormous fish. One great long fin ran under its belly in the water, but all the rest of it was raised above the surface. The Goldfish knew every fish in the sea, but he had never before seen such a fish as this! It was bigger than the Whale, and as black as the ink of the Octopus. He swam all round it, touching it with his inquisitive little nose. At last he asked,

'What sort of fish are *you?*'

The big black shadow laughed. 'I am not a fish at all, I am a ship.'

'What are you doing here if you are not a fish?'

'Just at present I am doing nothing, for I am becalmed. But when the wind blows I shall go on sailing round the world.'

'What is the world?'

'All that you see and more.'

'Am I in the world, then?' asked the Goldfish.

'Certainly you are.'

The Goldfish gave a little jump of delight. 'Good news! good news!' he cried.

A passing Porpoise paused to ask, 'What are you shouting for?'

'Because I am in the world!'

'Who says so?'

'The Ship-Fish!' said the Goldfish.

'Pooh!' said the Porpoise, 'let him prove it! and passed on.

The Goldfish stopped jumping, because his joy had been damped by doubt. 'How can the world be more than I can see?' he asked the Ship. 'If I am really in the world I ought to be able to see it *all*—or how can I be sure?'

'You must take my word for it,' said the Ship.

The Goldfish

'A tiny fellow like you can never hope to see more than a scrap of the world. The world has a rim you can never see over; the world has foreign lands full of wonders that you can never look upon; the world is as round as an orange, but you will never see how round the world is.'

Then the ship went on to tell of the parts of the world that lay beyond the rim of things, of men and women and children, of flowers and trees, of birds with eyes in their tails, blue, gold, and green, of white and black elephants, and temples hung with tinkling bells. The Goldfish wept with longing because he could never see over the rim of things, because he could not see how round the world was, because he could not behold all at once all the wonders that were in the world.

How the Ship laughed at him! 'My little friend,' said he, 'if you were the Moon yonder, why, if you were the Sun himself, you could only see one half of these things at a time.'

'Who is the Moon yonder?' asked the Goldfish.

'Who else but that silver slip of light up in the sky?'

'Is that the sky?' said the Goldfish. 'I thought it was another sea. And is that the Moon? I thought she was a Silver Fish. But who then is the Sun?'

'The Sun is the round gold ball that rolls through the sky by day,' said the Ship. 'They say he is her lover, and gives her his light.'

'But I will give her the world!' cried the Goldfish. And leaped with all his tiny might into the air, but he could not reach the Moon, and fell gasping into the sea. There he let himself sink like a little gold stone to the bottom of the ocean, where he lay for a week weeping his heart out. For the things the Ship had told him were more than he could understand; but they swelled him with great longings—longings to possess the Silver Moon, to be a mightier fish than the Sun, and to see the whole of the world from top to bottom and from side to side, with all the wonders within and beyond it.

Now it happened that King Neptune, who ruled the land under the waves, was strolling through a grove of white and scarlet coral, when he heard a chuckle that was something between a panting and puffing; and peering through the branches of the coral-trees he beheld a plump Porpoise bursting its sleek sides with laughter. Not far off lay the Goldfish, swimming in tears.

The Goldfish

King Neptune, like a good father, preferred to share in all the joys and sorrows of his children, so he stopped to ask the Porpoise, 'What tickles you so?'

'Ho! ho! ho!' puffed the Porpoise. 'I am tickled by the grief of the Goldfish there.'

'Has the Goldfish a grief?' asked King Neptune.

'He has indeed! For seven days and nights he has wept because, ho! ho! ho! because he cannot marry the Moon, surpass the Sun, and possess the world!'

'And you,' said King Neptune, 'have you never wept for these things?'

'Not I!' puffed the Porpoise. 'What! weep for the Sun and the Moon that are nothing but two blobs in the distance? Weep for the world that no one can behold? No, Father! When my dinner is in the distance, I'll weep for *that;* and when I see death coming, I'll weep for *that;* but for the rest, I say pooh!'

'Well, it takes all sorts of fish to make a sea,' said King Neptune, and stooping down he picked up the Goldfish and admonished it with his finger.

'Come, child,' said he, 'tears may be the beginning but they should not be the end of things. Tears will get you nowhere. Do you really wish to marry the Moon, surpass the Sun, and possess the world?

'I do, Father, I do! quivered the Goldfish.

'Then since there is no help for it, you must get caught in the net—do you see it floating yonder in the water? Are you afraid of it?'

'Not if it will bring me all I long for,' said the Goldfish bravely.

'Risk all, and you will get your desires,' promised King Neptune. He let the Goldfish dart through his fingers, and saw him swim boldly to the net which was waiting to catch what it could. As the meshes closed upon him, King Neptune stretched out his hand, and slipped a second fish inside it; and then, stroking his green beard, he continued his stroll among his big and little children.

And what happened to the Goldfish?

He was drawn up into the Fisherman's boat that lay in wait above the net; and in the same cast a Silver Fish was taken, a lovely creature with a round body and silky fins like films of moonlit cloud. 'There's a pretty pair!' thought the Fisherman, and he carried them home to please his little daughter. And to make her pleasure more complete, he first bought a globe of glass, and sprinkled sand and shells and tiny pebbles at the bottom, and set among them a sprig of coral and a strand of seaweed. Then he filled the globe with water, dropped in the Gold and Silver Fishes, and put the little glass world on a table in his cottage window.

The Goldfish, dazed with joy, swam towards the Silver Fish, crying, 'You are the Moon come out of the sky! Oh see, how round the world is!'

And he looked through one side of the globe, and saw flowers and trees in the garden; and he looked through another side of the globe, and saw on the mantelpiece black and white elephants of ebony and ivory, that the Fisherman had brought from foreign parts; and through another side of the globe he saw on the wall a fan of peacock's feathers, with eyes of gold and blue and green; and through the fourth side, on a bracket, he saw a little Chinese temple hung with bells. And he looked at the bottom of the globe, and saw his own familiar world of coral, sand, and shells. And he looked at the top of the globe, and saw a man, a woman, and a child smiling down at him over the rim.

And he gave a little jump of joy, and cried to his Silver Bride:

'Oh Moonfish, I am greater than the Sun! for

I give you, not half, but the whole of the world, the top and the bottom and all the way round, with all the wonders that are in it and beyond it!'

And King Neptune under the sea, who had ears for all that passed, laughed in his beard and said:

'It was a shame ever to let such a tiny fellow loose in the vast ocean. He needed a world more suited to his size.'

And ever since then, the world of the Goldfish has been a globe of glass.

THE JUNIOR GREAT BOOKS PROGRAM

ELEMENTS OF SHARED INQUIRY
A Short Course On
Interpretive Reading and Discussion

PART ONE

THE JUNIOR GREAT BOOKS PROGRAM

In the Junior Great Books Program, you read and discuss a number of selections, mostly stories but occasionally a play or a poem. Each reading has been chosen for three reasons: we believe you will enjoy it; we believe it has more meanings than any reader is likely to find on his or her own; and we believe that discussion of these meanings can affect the way you look at yourself, other people, and the world.

When we speak about the *meanings* of a selection, we are talking about its many possible interpretations, the different things the author wants us to think about or to feel through his or her words. Sometimes the search for these meanings may center on a single word. For example, in "The Happy Prince," the first story you read: Why does the Prince call the suffering of men and women "more marvelous than anything"? Usually, we think of "marvelous" as referring to strange or mysterious things we have never seen, such as the stories about foreign lands that the sparrow tells the Prince. Why then does the Prince think of something he sees every day in this way?

On other occasions, interpretation of a work may focus on a particular passage. For example: Why does the author have the Art Professor say that because the Happy Prince was no longer beautiful he was no longer useful? The author could have left out that remark. Why didn't he?

Finally, interpretation may cover many passages or even the work as a whole. For example: Why does the sparrow keep telling the Prince about Egypt? That question occurred to us again and again as we read different passages. Does the author want us to believe no one has the right to be happy while some people are unhappy? For us, that question asks about a possible meaning of the entire story.

In the Junior Great Books Program, it doesn't matter whether interpretation centers on a word, a passage, or the whole selection as long it helps us to figure out what the author is trying to tell us or make us feel.

Junior Great Books discussions are usually led by two people. Their job is to increase your understanding of what you have read by encouraging you to think for yourself about what it means. They conduct the discussion by asking questions that help to interpret the author's meaning. In addition to being interpretive, their questions have another important characteristic: they are questions to which the discussion leaders themselves are not sure of the answer. Often, this is because they think their questions can be answered correctly in more than one way, or they may not have found any answer that satisfies them, even after two careful readings of the selection. In either case, the discussion leaders share real questions of meaning with you and seek your help in answering them. For this reason, we call our method of discussion *shared inquiry*.

In shared inquiry, you are free to answer the discussion leaders' interpretive questions in any way that you like. You are equally free not to answer them at all if you have nothing to say at the moment. If you do answer the questions, the leaders may ask you to point out what it is in the story that makes you think your answer is correct. Other participants are free to agree or disagree with you, but they too may be asked to support their answers with evidence from the story. As a result of what your fellow participants say in the discussion, you may change your mind about how you interpret something in the story. Shared inquiry offers the opportunity to learn from the author *and* to learn from one another.

In shared inquiry, there are four rules. All of them are intended to help you interpret a selection by encouraging you to think for yourself about its meaning during a discussion.

Rule One. Discuss only the story, poem, or play that everyone has read. For your first meeting that will be "The Happy Prince". This rule gives everyone an equal opportunity to participate. No one is shut out of the discussion because references are made to other stories that he or she has not read.

Another reason for this rule is that by discussing only the story everyone has read, which you will have in front of you, you can decide whether other participants make accurate and appropriate references to the story in supporting their opinions about the author's meaning.

Rule Two. Do not introduce outside opinions—those of a teacher, parent, or editor, for example, to support your interpretation of the meaning of the story. In the Junior Great Books Program, the challenge in both reading and discussion is to figure out your own meaning of a written work. You support or prove the correctness of your opinions by finding evidence to back them up within the story or poem itself. You cannot state the opinions of other people and say "they must be correct because they know more about the story than I do." If you agree with an outside opinion, put it into your own words and present it as your opinion. Then, you must support it with evidence from the story just as if you had thought of it yourself.

Rule Three. No one may take part in the discussion who has not read the selection before the meeting. You are going to read works that are rich in meaning, usually with far more meaning than you will have time to discover. You have no time to waste listening to opinions about the meaning of a story by people who have not read it or who read it a long time ago. They are in no position to support their opinions with evidence from the story or to make a sound judgment about what someone else says about it.

Rule Four. The leaders of the discussion may ask questions but not answer them. If the discussion leaders could answer questions, you might begin to feel that you didn't have to think for yourself. If you were temporarily stuck on a question, you could forget about it because you would know the leaders would eventually answer it. Allowing the discussion leaders only to *ask* questions means that you must take major responsibility for what you learn in the discussion.

"SLOW" READING IN SHARED INQUIRY

The First Reading

As we read a story, most of us divide our time between trying to follow the action and deciding whether or not we like it. We spend little or no time trying to figure out what the story means, what the author is trying to tell us or make us feel through his words. It is important to recall and to evaluate what we read. But if we do not try to interpret a story, we lose the pleasure of discovering meaning for ourselves; and we lose the opportunity to apply that meaning to our own lives. In the Junior Great Books Program, the stress is on interpretation: helping you to develop the habit of asking continually, "I wonder what the author means by that?"

Interpretation begins with your own first reading of a selection. During the first reading, your main concern should be to get down in writing as many *responses* as possible to the selection. By responses we mean all the questions, thoughts, and feelings you have about the author's words. These may take the form of underlining passages, writing comments, or putting question marks in the margin. How you do it doesn't matter. What is important is that you make a note of your responses. It is hard to keep responses in your head. It is still harder to try to connect responses or to turn them into questions if you don't write them down. Therefore, in preparation for shared inquiry, you should always read with pencil or pen in hand.

As you read, your responses may come from several

sources. One is words or passages you don't understand. If the word is a new one for you, look up its meaning in a dictionary and write it down on the page of the story where the word appears. Usually, however, the words you are puzzled about will be familiar ones. The difficulty is in deciding how the author is using them in the story. In "The Elephant's Child," an example of such a phrase for us is: " 'satiable curtiosity." Ordinarily, we try to write every word correctly. Why then does the author purposely drop the first two letters of "insatiable" and misspell "curiosity" every time the words appear in the story?

Words or passages that you think are important are a second source of responses. For example, you might underline the passage in which we learn that the fourth advantage of the elephant's trunk is that it is useful to spank people with. The author could have mentioned only the first three advantages of the elephant's trunk. As you first read a story, you don't have to think about *why* something is important. You can find the reasons later. Just be sure to mark the passage so you don't forget it.

Your own feelings toward some of the author's words provide a third source of responses. You like or don't like a particular passage; you agree or disagree strongly with something the author says; or the words remind you of your own experience. We thought it was unfair for the Elephant's Child to be spanked by his family every time he asks a question. We wondered why the author had the Elephant's Child's curiosity treated in this way. Again, at this stage it is more important to note your feelings in writing than it is to explain them.

A final source of responses may be connections you see between passages or sections in the story. For example, we noted in the margin of our book that the Snake not only helps the Elephant's Child but also keeps explaining things to him. We were curious why the author didn't have the Elephant's Child figure out the advantages of his trunk for himself. Whenever you begin to see possible connections, mark them in your book.

Just as no one can tell you what your interpretation of the selections in the Junior Great Books Program should be, no one can tell what responses you should have as you are reading or which passages you should find important, puzzling, or related to each other. These responses will vary from reader to reader. But all of them may be useful in helping you to discover the author's meaning either on a page or in the work as a whole.

For the next meeting, note your responses for "Messenger to Maftam" and "The Cow-Tail Switch" as you are reading them. Then look over your responses to see whether they lead to questions about the meaning of the selection you would like to discuss. Write several of these questions out. The leaders will try to save a few minutes at the end of the meeting to discuss some of them.

EXERCISE 1

Printed below is a passage from "The Elephant's Child" that includes some of the responses we noted as we read it. Just for practice, see how many of these responses you can change into questions about the author's meaning. For example, the sentences we bracketed led to the question Why does the author show us again the advantages of the Elephant's trunk?

*Elephant's → * "So the Elephant's Child went home across Africa
child never   *made to sound like him*
given a
name   frisking and whisking his trunk. When he wanted

advantages   fruit to eat he pulled fruit down from a tree, instead
mentioned
on   of waiting for it to fall as he used to do. When he
previous
page   wanted grass he plucked grass up from the ground,

                          new piece of information
                 instead of going on his knees as he used to do. When

                 the flies bit him he broke off the branch of a tree and

                 used it as a fly-whisk; and he made himself a new

                 cool, slushy-squashy mud-cap whenever the sun was
                          a new advantage
                 hot. When he <u>felt lonely walking</u> through Africa he

                 sang to himself <u>down his trunk</u> and the noise was

                 louder than several brass bands. He went especially

out of his way to find a broad Hippopotamus (she was no [?] relation of his), and he spanked her very hard to make sure that the Bi-Coloured-Python-Rock-Snake had spoken the truth about his new trunk.

[annotations: "a long description instead of giving her a short name or calling her Python."]

The rest of the time he picked up the melon rinds that he had dropped on his way to Limpopo—for he was a Tidy Pachyderm." [annotation: "a more difficult word for elephant."]

"SLOW" READING IN SHARED INQUIRY

The Second Reading

You begin to interpret a story on the first reading by writing your responses in the margins. But we recommend a second reading for several reasons. One is the influence of the element of suspense. The first time you read a story, you may be so eager to know how it turns out that it will become difficult to stop and mark your responses. During a second reading, you will be more likely to consider what the author is trying to make you think or feel as the story moves along. Second, in light of the whole selection, you may find new passages to respond to—passages that you think are important or that you don't understand. For example, during the first reading of "The Messenger to Maftam", we were surprised to find Mawadi still qualifying everything he said after he proved to Bahene that he never told a lie. That made us wonder whether the author wanted us to believe Mawadi deserved his reputation for honesty. As we reread the story we especially looked for passages that would help us to answer this question.

Third, having read the story once, you may be able to find connections between one part and another part that were impossible to catch before. During our second reading of "The Messenger to Maftam" we noticed that Bahene mentions several times that cleverness or wisdom, as well as virtue, is needed always to tell the truth. Does the author want us to agree with Bahene, or does he want us to believe that only cleverness is needed to gain a reputation for never making a false statement?

Fourth, during a second reading, you can think about your original responses. Some of the questions you had will have been answered by later passages in the story; others will remain real questions for you. Some passages that you underlined will now strike you as more important than others. In looking at them again, questions may occur to you about what they mean.

Noting your responses and going back over them to see how many can be turned into questions about the author's intention means taking seriously your own thoughts and feelings about a story. Many people look immediately to some expert to tell them what a story means because they have no confidence in their ability to figure it out for themselves. The views of experts are useful and necessary, but they are no substitute for thinking for yourself, for gaining a respect for your own responses.

We call the manner of reading for shared inquiry "slow" reading because we think the word stresses something important. We are not saying that all written material should be read slowly. We ask you to read the works in the Junior Great Books Program slowly, in the ways we have outlined, because otherwise you will miss too much in them that is worth thinking about and discussing.

Continue to jot down your responses for each selection as you are reading or rereading it. After your second reading, try to turn some of the comments you have made or passages you have underlined or been puzzled about into questions concerning the author's meaning. The leaders will try to take up a few of these questions after the regular discussions.

"Slow" Reading in Shared Inquiry

EXERCISE 2

"The Cow-Tail Switch"

Listed below are some of the questions about the author's meaning that we thought of after our second reading of "The Cow-Tail Switch". Jot down a brief answer to each question and then compare your answer to that of other members of your group. We think each question can be answered correctly in more than one way.

1. Why does the Author make Puli's first words "Where is Father"?

    Your answer:_____

    _____

2. Why don't the older sons think of looking for their father again until Puli asks for him?

    Your answer:_____

    _____

3. Why did a different son find the trail each time?

    Your answer:_____

    _____

4. Why did each son have a different power to help bring his father back to life?

    Your answer:_____

5. Why are the powers of all the sons needed to bring their father back to life?

   Your answer: _____

6. Why does the author want us to know that Ogaloussa wasn't the only one who ever came back from the dead?

   Your answer: _____

7. Why does the author have the villagers as well as the sons argue about who deserves the cow-tail switch?

   Your answer: _____

8. Why does the author include a saying that supports Ogaloussa's decision?

   Your answer: _____

QUESTIONS OF INTERPRETATION, FACT, AND EVALUATION

In the last section, we spoke about the importance of noting your responses to a selection in writing. If all these responses were turned into questions, you would probably have examples of three kinds of questions you could ask about a story in shared inquiry. These are questions of interpretation, questions of fact, and questions of evaluation.

Questions of interpretation ask you to give your opinion about the author's meaning and to support your opinion with evidence from the selection. Answers to questions of interpretation depend on more than just memory. The author doesn't usually explain why there are certain scenes or actions in the story. You have to figure out the reasons for yourself. And because people can read the same lines and come to different conclusions about what they mean, most questions of interpretation have more than one possible answer. Example: In "The Bat, The Birds, and The Beasts", why didn't the Bat join one of the armies? Some participants may think that the Bat was confused about what kind of creature he was. Others may think the Bat was afraid and wanted to avoid the conflict.

Questions of fact ask you to recall something the author said. In contrast to questions of interpretation, questions of fact are usually answered from memory and have only one possible answer.

In shared inquiry, we consider a fact to be any statement made by the author. It is a fact in "The Bat, The Birds, and The Beasts" that the Bat didn't try to join either side until peace was made. This statement is a fact not because you approve of the Bat's actions but because the author says it. A question of fact asks you to recall something the author said either in your own words or by reading from the selection. Example: How do the Birds and the Beasts treat the Bat when he tries to join their celebration? Answer: Both the Birds and the Beasts throw him out.

Questions of evaluation ask you to consider whether you agree or disagree with what the author says or means on the basis of your own experiences, likes and dislikes, or beliefs. Example: Do you believe you can lose your friends if you don't take sides in arguments between them?

If you can't decide whether a question is one of fact, interpretation, or evaluation, start to answer the question yourself for about thirty seconds. Notice where you begin to look for an answer. If you are looking for an anwer inside the selection you have read, the question is either interpretive or factual. If you think two people might disagree about the answer, and if you think each could support a different answer with evidence from the story, then the question is interpretive. If you think there is only one possible answer to the question, and little or no explanation is needed to prove that your answer is correct (sometimes just pointing to the author's words is enough), the question is factual.

EXERCISE 3

"The Hare with Many Friends"

For each of the following questions, write (F) if the question is FACTUAL; (I) if the question is INTERPRETIVE; and (E) if the question is EVALUATIVE.

____ 1. Why does each of the animals give a reason why he can't help the Hare?

____ 2. Does the Hare escape from the hounds?

____ 3. Do you believe you can have too many friends?

____ 4. Why do most of the animals suggest that someone else will help the Hare?

____ 5. Who is the last animal the Hare seeks help from?

____ 6. Why does the author have the Hare seek help from different kinds of animals?

____ 7. Which animals are worried about the danger to their own life if they help the Hare?

____ 8. What have you found is the best test of friendship?

____ 9. If you were in trouble, would you seek help from a friend or depend on yourself to get out of it?

____10. Why does Aesop have the Hare escape instead of getting caught by the hounds?

THE USES OF QUESTIONS OF INTERPRETATION, FACT, AND EVALUATION

Questions of interpretation, fact, and evaluation all play a part in shared inquiry, but they are not of equal importance. Interpretive questions are the most important. The purpose of shared inquiry is to teach you to *interpret* what you read by encouraging you to think for yourself about the author's meaning.

Factual questions are the next most important. The discussion leaders must ask them continually to get participants to support their opinions about meaning with facts from the story.

Questions of evaluation are the least important in shared inquiry. Most of your time will be needed to discover as much of the author's meaning as you can. For this reason, usually there is little opportunity for questions of evaluation—discussing whether or not you agree with the author or like or believe what he says.

EXERCISE 4

"The Owl Who Was God"

Here is another exercise to help you learn the differences between questions of interpretation, fact, and evaluation. Remember: A question of *fact* asks what the author said and has one answer. A question of *interpretation* asks what the author means and usually can be answered in different ways. A question of *evaluation* asks about you—your experiences, your beliefs, or your likes and dislikes. For each of the following questions, write (F) if the question is FACTUAL; (I) if the question if INTERPRETIVE; and (E) if the question if EVALUATIVE.

____ 1. When the Owl is on the highway, why does the author have him repeat two of the words he said at night?

____ 2. What makes the animals decide the Owl is God?

____ 3. What happens to the Fox and his friends?

____ 4. What qualities would you look for in a leader?

____ 5. Why does the author have the Fox and his friends ask if the Owl can see in the daytime?

____ 6. Have you ever found appearances to be deceiving?

____ 7. Do the Owl's followers doubt that he is God up until the time that the truck hits them?

The Uses of Questions 189

_____ 8. Does your behavior change in a crowd?

_____ 9. Why does the author have the Owl asked a series of questions before he is declared to be great and wise?

_____10. Does the author want us to believe the Owl is saying the same word in answer to each question?

WRITING GOOD PREPARED QUESTIONS

We suggested that you try to write some questions of your own for each selection. In this section, we want to talk about the qualities your prepared questions should have.

The first quality of questions you write for discussion is that they should be interpretive. Interpretive questions provide you with ways to explore the author's meaning, which is the purpose of shared inquiry.

The second quality you should look for in your prepared questions is your own doubt about the answers. The questions should be ones you can't answer at all or that you think can be answered correctly in more than one way, and you are not sure which is the best way.

Although you should have some doubt about the answers to your prepared questions, you should be fairly certain that they can be answered by discussing the selection everyone has read. If they can't, participants will either say nothing or express a lot of opinions that can't be pinned down with evidence from the selection.

In addition, good prepared questions should be specific. Questions that are specific show someone immediately what the problem of interpretation is for you in the selection. They are questions that only someone who has read the selection carefully could write. Specific questions do not mean questions that take up trivial points in a selection. They shoul deal with what you consider to be important problems of interpretation. For us, an example of such a question about "The Story of Dr. Dolittle" would be: Why does the author make money a nuisance for Dr. Dolittle? We see the question leading to a discussion of many ideas including, "Why do the animals worry more about money than Dr. Dolittle does?" "Why does money make Dr. Dolittle return from Africa to Puddleby?" and, "Why does the author have Dr. Dolittle end up rich?"

The trouble with questions that are not specific—that could be asked about many selections—is that they don't make you think right away about possible answers. Take the question, "What's the main theme of the story?" or "What is the author's attitude toward the characters in his story?"

You could ask these questions about "The Cow-Tail Switch" or about any other story for that matter. Such questions make it hard to think, just as vague directions make it hard to act. Imagine trying to keep a date with a friend who said, "Meet me downtown on Saturday afternoon."

The final quality of prepared questions is that they should be clear. All good questions should be readily understood by someone who has read the work. The energy of your fellow participants should be spent in trying to answer interpretive questions, not in trying to figure out what they mean. Unclear questions waste time and they can make participants feel stupid. Let's say someone asked this question about "The Story of Dr. Dolittle": Does animalistic behavior actually reveal more attributes associated with maturation than Dr. Dolittle displays? The question is confusing and no one will understand the problem. But if you worded the same question clearly "Do the animals act more grown-up than Dr. Dolittle?" most participants would be able to start to answer it and would be interested in hearing what the others had to say.

Writing Good Prepared Questions

EXERCISE 5

"The Story of Dr. Dolittle"

Many of the questions in this exercise lack one of the qualities of good questions. Decide which statement below best describes each question and then place the appropriate letter next to it.

    A) Question is not clear

    B) Question is not specific enough

    C) No doubt about the answer to the question

    D) Question is not answerable from the selection

    E) Question is satisfactory

____ 1. Why are the characters given the names they have?

____ 2. Did Sarah Dolittle get married?

____ 3. Why is extinction and uniqueness of the pushmi-pullyu posited before the appearance of the creature?

____ 4. Why does the story end as it does?

____ 5. In the story, do the animals admire Dr. Dolittle more than most of the people do?

Writing Good Prepared Questions 193

____ 6. Why does the author have some of the animals keep house for Dr. Dolittle?

____ 7. Will Dr. Dolittle return to Africa?

____ 8. Why does Dr. Dolittle lose most of his human patients?

____ 9. Is Dr. Dolittle's name intended to suggest incompetency according to a standard the author finds invalid?

____10. Why does the author make most of the people in the story less likeable than the animals?

TEXTUAL ANALYSIS

Even if you have a good memory, you have probably found it necessary during the discussion to read some passage again either to answer a question about it or to check the soundness of someone else's answer. These are good reasons for always having the selection you are discussing right in front of you. Another is that having the selection there gives you a chance to do textual analysis. By textual analysis, we mean a detailed examination of a particular passage in which you try to determine the author's meaning line by line and sometimes word by word.

This activity may be carried on as a way of getting into a selection when the group has not read well enough to explore an interpretive question. Textual analysis is also valuable when a group is interpreting a work satisfactorily and has a number of ideas about what a work means. In this situation, textual analysis is a way of using the ideas already expressed to extract more meaning from particular passages, meanings that may help to answer an interpretive question satisfactorily.

    Step A. Find the passage that you want to examine closely and have someone in the group read it aloud. Even if it is difficult, you may get some new sense of what it is about.

    Step B. Identify who is talking. It may be the author speaking to you directly, a fictitious narrator, or one of the characters speaking to another character.

Step C. If you choose some passage other than the beginning, try to get a rough idea of where you are in the selection. Look briefly at the page or two before the passage to help refresh your memory.

Step D. This step is the most important one. Go over the difficult passage, line by line. Ask any questions about the meaning of words, phrases, and sentences to which you are not sure of the answer. If you are called on to answer questions that someone else has about a line, try to put your response into your own words instead of using the words of the author. If you simply repeat what the author says, you may not really understand his or her meaning. Feel free to turn to other sections of the work that you think will help you answer questions about the passage you are examining closely. No one can tell you specifically what passages to turn to, but they are usually passages dealing with the same ideas, often expressed in the same words.

Textual Analysis

EXERCISE 6

"The Goldfish"

To find out how textual analysis works, see how many questions you can ask and answer for the following passage from "The Goldfish". We have suggested a few questions. See whether you can think of others.

> "King Neptune, like a good father, preferred to share in all the joys and sorrows of his children, so he stopped to ask the Porpoise, 'What tickles you so?'
>
> 'Ho! ho! ho!' puffed the Porpoise. 'I am tickled by the grief of the Goldfish there.'
>
> 'Has the Goldfish a grief?' asked King Neptune.
>
> 'He has indeed! For seven days and nights he has wept because, ho! ho! ho! because he cannot marry the Moon, surpass the Sun, and possess the world!'
>
> 'And you,' said King Neptune, 'have never wept for these things?'
>
> 'Not I!' puffed the Porpoise. 'What! weep for the Sun and the Moon that are nothing but two blobs in the distance? Weep for the world that no one can behold? No, Father! When my dinner is in the distance, I'll weep for *that*; and when I see death coming, I'll weep for *that*; but for the rest, I say pooh!'
>
> 'Well, it takes all sorts of fish to make a sea,' said King

Textual Analysis

Neptune, and stooping down he picked up the Goldfish and admonished it with his finger."

1. Who is King Neptune?

2. Why is the Goldfish sad?

3. Why does the author have the Porpoise find the Goldfish's grief humorous?

4. Why does the author have King Neptune find out about the Goldfish's grief from the Porpoise?

5. Why does the author make something as small as the Goldfish so ambitious?

6. Does the author want us to agree with the Porpoise that it is foolish to weep for the sun, the moon, and the world?

7. Does the author want us to agree with the Porpoise that food and death are most important?

8. Why would the Porpoise weep for his dinner "in the distance"?

9. Why is the word "puffed" used twice to describe the way the Porpoise talks?

10. If the author doesn't want us to agree with the Porpoise, why does the story include his views?

11. Why does King Neptune ask the Porpoise whether he

has ever wept for the things that the Goldfish wants?

12. Why does King Neptune say "it takes all sorts of fish to make up the sea" instead of stating his own opinions about what is important?